A Beautiful Stranger . . .

"You're gorgeous!" Robert hissed in my ear. "But who's that with you?"

I shrugged at Robert to indicate I didn't know who my partner was. Both Robert and the wolf man, I noticed, were looking at me with curiosity and intense interest.

I put my hand on Roddy's arm and smiled with my luscious hot-pink lips. As the old Glenda, I was still mad at Roddy from our last encounter. But tonight I wasn't really that Glenda. I was a mysterious, masked, dance-hall queen whom Roddy didn't recognize. And somehow I didn't feel like *me* at all.

Hey, Remember Fat Glenda?

by Lila Perl

AN ARCHWAY PAPERBACK
Published by POCKET BOOKS • NEW YORK

An Archway Paperback published by
POCKET BOOKS, a Simon & Schuster division of
GULF & WESTERN CORPORATION
1230 Avenue of the Americas, New York, N.Y. 10020

Published by arrangement with Houghton Mifflin/Clarion Books
Library of Congress Catalog Card Number: 80-28258

ISBN: 0-671-44954-0

First Archway Paperback printing November, 1982

10 9 8 7 6 5 4 3 2 1

AN ARCHWAY PAPERBACK and colophon are
trademarks of Simon & Schuster.

Printed in the U.S.A.

IL 5+

For Diane—
who first introduced me
to Fat Glenda, and for all
those readers who wanted
to meet her again

Hey, Remember
Fat Glenda?

1

"He–e–e–y–y, Jelly Belly!"

Someone had just gone whizzing past me on a bike. Whammo. The words hit me like a fast jab in the stomach.

I cut my jogging pace and caught my breath long enough to scream back, "Hey, you!"

Then I stopped running altogether and looked around me. Maybe the kid on the bike hadn't been calling out to me, maybe he hadn't even *said*, "Jelly Belly."

But deep down something told me he had. Because, you see, when you've been fat as long as I have you just naturally expect to be teased a lot and called nasty names.

The really unfair part was that I'd been dieting all summer, and for a long time before that. But the summer was the part I was proudest of. I'd lost sixteen pounds, nearly two pounds a week. And I was doing it all by mail.

In fact, I was on my way to the mailbox when that kid yelled out to me. Not to the nearest mailbox, either, but to the one that was about twelve blocks away from our house, way over on the other side of Havenhurst, this town out on Long Island where I live.

How can you lose weight by mail? Well, jogging to and from the mailbox is only part of it. I was also writing to Sara Mayberry, my best and, I sometimes think, only friend in the whole world.

Sara had lived just down the street from me in Havenhurst for nearly a year while her father had a teaching job at a nearby college. Now she and her family were back in California. Sara wasn't fat. In fact, she was sort of skinny. But she'd had other kinds of problems when she'd lived in Havenhurst, and she had understood my problems better than anybody.

When she moved back to California in June, we both cried so much that we filled up two tiny little perfume-sample bottles with our mixed-together tears, and we vowed to keep them forever. We also promised to keep writing each other till we died. And Sara made me another promise.

"Glenda, I promise to keep on helping you to lose weight. Because I'll still be your friend and even from three thousand miles away I'll exert all my powers to make you think skinny and eat less and exercise more, and most of all, to be happy so you don't go on eating binges to drown your sorrows."

Sara had even written me a little poem before she

left. It didn't rhyme too well, but still I thought it was perfect. It went:

> *Just start shedding pounds*
> *And folks'll soon wonder,*
> *Whatever became of . . .*
> > *Fat Glenda?*

Can you understand how wonderful it was to have a friend like that and how terrible it was for her to move away, probably forever?

When I started up jogging again and finally arrived huffing and puffing at the mailbox with the letter I was sending to Sara, I felt like writing a *p.s.* on the envelope and telling her that somebody had just called me "Jelly Belly" even though there were sixteen pounds *less* of flab on me now, at the beginning of September, than there had been in June.

I was especially supposed to write Sara the things that made me unhappy because she'd noticed long ago that:

> *Every time*
> *You take a beating,*
> *You try to make it up*
> > *By eating.*

Sara had kept on sending me rhymes like that in the mail. She sent them on big pieces of colored construction paper that I tacked up in my room.

But today I didn't have a pen or a pencil with me

for a *p.s.*, so I just popped the letter into the box and decided I'd write her about my latest insult next time. Maybe by then I'd even know who it was who'd yelled out to me.

Was it one of the old crowd who'd tried to make my life miserable in seventh grade or somebody new from eighth grade, which had just started a few days ago? I had been really dreading starting a whole new school year in junior high without Sara. I guess that was one of the reasons I'd worked so hard at getting thinner all summer.

But not thin enough. Not *nearly* thin enough.

My mother, of course, didn't see it that way at all. It wasn't that she didn't *want* me to lose weight. She just didn't approve of my jogging all over the neighborhood. She wanted me to take an exercise class at a regular studio like she did.

The minute I reached home and saw my mother's car in the driveway, I knew the argument was going to start up all over again. There was no way for me to sneak past her, get to my room at the opposite end of the house, and take a shower without her knowing I'd been out running.

"Oh, GLENN-da," she said the moment she saw me. Her mouth and even her eyes seemed to turn down at the edges with disappointment. "Just *look* at you. You're wringing wet and red as a beet."

"Sure," I said breezily, trying to inch past her. There wasn't much room though because she had the refrigerator door wide open, and my mother wasn't exactly slender herself. She seemed to be trying to make up her mind about something to eat.

"And that jogging suit," she said, closing the door and deciding to concentrate on me instead. "I don't know why they can't make those things to look a little more stylish."

"The suit's fine," I replied. "You even said it was okay when we bought it."

"Yes, I know," she said. Then, brightening up suddenly, she added, "Maybe you won't be using it much after all."

"Why not? I still have plenty of weight to lose."

"Yes, but I've got some very interesting news. I ran into Miss Esme Aurelio in town today. You remember Miss Esme, Glenda. She had that dance studio in Havenhurst upstairs from the old post office when you were a little girl. You weren't old enough then to take lessons."

"Oh, no," I said quickly. "I don't want to take dancing lessons. It's embarrassing. When I'm thin enough, I'll just . . . well, I'll just naturally learn to dance. All the kids do it that way. Nobody actually takes lessons nowadays."

"That's because there aren't any steps to learn, just twitching your hips and jerking your shoulders," my mother sniffed. "But hold on a minute. I'm not talking about dancing lessons. I'm talking about *dancercises*. Get it? *Dance exercises*. Sit down a minute, baby. I want to talk to you about it."

I ran my fingers through my hair, which felt both crinkly and damp, and prepared to slump down at the kitchen table. I knew I'd have to hear all about it right now whether I wanted to or not.

My mother opened the refrigerator door and took out a small cup of banana yogurt. "Want one, honey?"

"Nope. All I'm having is water."

She got a spoon and sat down across from me. "Now," she said, removing the lid from the yogurt container and carefully spooning up the extra yogurt that coated the underside, "Miss Esme is opening up a brand new studio to teach these wonderful classes. All the exercises are especially designed to slim and shape the body, and they're all done to music. No boring counting, and you don't get nearly so tired. You can just go on and on. Like dancing. As soon as she has ten people she'll start. *And* the first five will get a twenty-five percent discount. What do you think of that?"

I shook my head from side to side. "I'd rather just keep on jogging. And dieting, of course." I could just see myself being dragged to one of Miss Esme's classes with my mother and three or four of her overweight friends. I could just see them all cooing over me like I was the baby elephant of the herd and telling me how well I was doing. In the end I'd grow up to be exactly like them, still fat and still going to exercise classes just the way my mother had been doing all her life. I had to do this my way. Or rather the way Sara had helped me figure out to do it.

"Oh, honestly," my mother said, lapping up her yogurt. "I don't see how you can be so stubborn. You could at least try the dancercises for a while. Miss Esme

6

is especially geared to teaching young people. In fact, she plans to have a teen group, or maybe several. There are plenty of girls in this town who could use some slimming and trimming and at the same time learn to be a little more graceful. I'm sure you could get some of your friends to join."

I shook my head again. "I don't have any friends. Now that Sara's gone."

"Oh, Sara, Sara," my mother mumbled, scraping the bottom and sides of the yogurt cup clean with her spoon. "It's time to make some new friends. You would, Glenda, if you'd just get *into* something. Jogging all alone . . . well, aside from making a spectacle of yourself around Havenhurst, it just isn't the same as a well-designed body-shaping program."

I was sure those were Miss Esme's words and not my mother's.

"Do you know what happens to your body fat when you jog?" my mother continued. "Why all you do is to shake it up, until it becomes all quivery and jiggly. Just like a bowl of . . . jelly."

I sprang up from the table. Jelly! The next thing I knew my own mother would be calling me "Jelly Belly."

Tears were beginning to prickle at my eyelids.

"I've got to take a shower right now because I'm *awfully* hot," I gasped. And I lumbered out of the kitchen as fast as I could.

"Oh, Sara," I sighed, slamming the door of my room and starting to get out of my jogging suit. "You'd understand if only you were here. I know you would."

Just as if Sara had heard my thoughts, she answered

7

me with one of her most reassuring verse poems, the
one that I'd tacked up on the wall right over my bed:

> *Remember Glenda,*
> *I have no doubt*
> *There's a thin you inside*
> *That will get out!*

2

"Select a love poem of your choice from the anthology. Tell why you picked it and be prepared to discuss it in class. Write a short paragraph giving the sense of the poem in your own words."

It was the next evening. I had just sat down to do my homework, and I was reading over, for the first time, the copy of the assignment sheet that Mr. Hartley, our eighth-grade English teacher, had given out with the English textbooks that morning in class.

A love poem! I could feel my cheeks getting flushed, something I usually hated because when they got rosy and shiny they made my face look fatter than ever. I was glad I was all by myself in my room.

Mr. Hartley—Mr. *D.* Hartley—had been in my mind, sort of, ever since classes had begun earlier that week. It wasn't just because he was a man teacher. I'd had a man teacher for science in seventh grade. It was because he was a different *kind* of man teacher.

9

The first time I'd walked into the English room and seen him standing near the blackboard talking to a bunch of ninth-grade girls from the class before ours, I couldn't believe my eyes. He could have been a double for some of my favorite TV and movie actors. He was stunningly built, and his eyes were the most piercing, romantic blue I'd ever seen. The first thing I did was to drop into the nearest front row seat, which I would get to keep for the rest of the school year. That way, I'd be able to get in and out of the room as quickly as possible without his noticing—maybe—how much there was of me. You see, fat people think about things like that.

Was Mr. Hartley going to turn out to be as interesting and exciting as he looked? Usually, even the young, good-looking man teachers turned out to be as dry as dust, boring and fussy, worse even than some of the crotchety women teachers.

Slowly, I opened my English textbook. It had stories and essays and poems, lots of poems.

"A love poem," I whispered, turning the pages as though they were made out of lace. "What does he mean?"

I answered myself. "A poem about love, dummy. How hard can that be to find? Most poems are probably about love. I'll bet he *is* a very romantic person, just exactly the way he looks . . ."

A sharp rap at the door of my room startled me. I pulled my fingers away so quickly from the page I was holding that I nearly tore it. The next moment the doorknob turned with a very loud squeak and my mother was half inside the room.

"Glenda, didn't you hear me calling you? Someone's on the telephone, one of your school chums I think."

She followed me to the extension phone in her bedroom. "Find out if she'd be interested in dancercises," she hissed, as I picked up the receiver.

I waved my hand to brush her away, hoping whoever it was hadn't heard her. Then I waited a moment as she went on back to the den where she and my father were watching television.

"Hi," I said. "Who's this?"

"Who'd you think?" came a thin, teasing voice with a faint trace of a Southern accent.

"Oh, Mary Lou," I said, not exactly thrilled.

Mary Lou Blenheim had been living in Havenhurst for about two years and she had been in my class since sixth grade, but we weren't exactly friends. Last year she'd pulled a couple of nasty little tricks trying to get Sara away from me. And she'd also been friendly with a boy named Roddy Fenton, who had been one of my worst enemies. Not only had I had a whole lot of trouble with him, but he, too, had tried to bust up my friendship with Sara. I just *hoped* he wasn't the one who'd called me "Jelly Belly" the other day.

"So, Mary Lou," I said hesitatingly, "what's up? How come you're calling?"

"My," Mary Lou said, "you don't sound a bit friendly. I honestly do think, Glenda, that you're one of those people that nurses grudges. I waved to you in the schoolyard the other day, and you didn't even see me."

"Is that what you called me about? There must have been four thousand people all screaming and waving their hands around in that yard."

11

I felt like adding that Mary Lou's arm would be pretty hard to spot in the first place because it was so milky-white and skinny. Everything about Mary Lou was pale, her long limp white-blonde hair, her pasty complexion, and her long arms and legs. She was the complete opposite of me. My hair was reddish-blonde, short and thick, and crinkly-curly. I had freckles all over my cheeks, and my arms and legs were rosy-colored sausages compared to Mary Lou's spaghetti sticks.

To tell the truth, I wasn't exactly comfortable about going around in school with Mary Lou because seeing us together kids would just naturally think of "fat and skinny." And eating lunch with Mary Lou was worst of all because she had the tiniest little appetite and was a very picky eater. She thought most food was "disgustin'," her favorite word.

"Now listen here," Mary Lou replied, "I didn't call you to pick a bone or anything like that, Glenda, so no need getting irritated. What I actually called you about is the English assignment that Mr. Hartley gave out today."

"Oh," I said, getting a funny little twinge in my stomach at the mention of Mr. Hartley's name. "I was just looking it over. I was wondering if he wants us to pick a real romantic love poem."

"What do you think, Glenda?" Mary Lou asked. "I'm feeling sort of queasy about it. Talking about *love* with all those stupid boys in the class. And then there's Mr. Hartley himself. He's dreamy, though, don't you think?"

"Um hmmm," I agreed.

12

"You sit right in the front row, Glenda. I noticed you're always looking up at him, just gazing . . ."

"Well, of course," I said. "I'm supposed to. He's the teacher. Where else should I look?"

"But those eyes," Mary Lou sighed. "Don't they just *bore* through you, like blue flames?"

"Um hmmm. Except he's usually looking past me. Over toward the back of the room. Where you sit."

"I know," Mary Lou said. "But I can't always tell if he's looking at me or Cathanne or Patty. We all three sit back there. Maybe I need glasses. No, maybe not. If I actually *saw* him looking into my eyes, I'd die. I'd just die."

"Oh, Mary Lou, really."

"Well, I just don't know how you stand it. Being so close to him and all. Maybe you just have a stronger stomach than I do, Glenda. Oh," she added quickly, "I didn't mean anything by that. You understand. It's just that I faint so easily."

"Oh, sure," I said. I'd never actually seen Mary Lou faint, but I'd heard her scream and get hysterical if she saw a worm on the sidewalk or found a tiny bug crawling on her lettuce leaf. "Well, what about the love poem," I asked her. "Did you pick one yet?"

"No, did you? I'll never be able to do it. Cathanne found one and she dared me to use it. It goes, 'Come live with me, and be my love.' It's a poem by a 'passionate shepherd.' Isn't that embarrassing? I wouldn't take such a dare. Oh, what'll I do?"

"Pick something else. There are plenty of poems to choose from."

"Yeah," Mary Lou said downheartedly. "Oh, but I'm so dumb. I was thinking maybe you could help me, Glenda. Cathanne and Patty are such teases. The assignment isn't due until next Tuesday. Maybe we could get together over the weekend and work on it. What do you think?"

Just then I heard my mother coming out of the den. She was probably on her way to the kitchen for a snack. She'd been urging me to make new friends now that Sara was gone. Maybe this was my chance to get in with Mary Lou and the others.

"Okay," I said quickly. "Fine."

We set a day and a time for Mary Lou to come over.

A few minutes after I hung up and went back to my room, my mother poked her head in the door. She was carrying a plate of diet ice cream.

"Want some?" she asked, extending a spoonful. "It's coco-mocha flavor, only sixty-five calories a half-cup. You'd never guess it wasn't the real thing."

I was just about to open my mouth wide like I'd been doing practically all my life when I thought about Sara's warning. It was on bright poison-green construction paper, and I'd Scotch-taped it to the refrigerator door until my mother made me take it down because she said it was making her "nervous."

I shook my head no and pointed to the poem which now hung right above my desk:

A moment on the lips,
Forever on the hips.

My mother paid no attention and put the spoonful of ice cream in her own mouth instead.

"What a long conversation. Did you ask your friend about the dancercises? Who was that anyway?"

"Mary Lou Blenheim," I replied. "She's the skinniest person alive and she eats less than anyone I know. If she ever tried to do exercises, she'd probably fall down dead from malnutrition."

"Ah," my mother said, pointing the licked-off spoon at me, "there's where you're wrong, baby. Exercise would stimulate her appetite. And I'll tell you something else it would do. It would give her some curves, probably fill out her chest and give her shapely legs with nice curving calf muscles."

My mother kicked up one of her own legs and stroked her calf with her free hand. Her legs *were* sort of curvy, but they were definitely too fat. And in spite of all her exercise classes, her thighs were downright flabby.

My mother, she had an answer for everything!

Later that evening I started a letter to Sara.

Things are pretty much the same around here. My mother took the "moment on the lips, forever on the hips" sign down from the refrigerator door and now she's eating stuff between meals like always. But I've been refusing to share snacks with her, and I'm going to keep my promise not to have anything between meals except water. No more diet sodas either. Like you said, they just keep you in the mood for sweet things and they have all those bad chemicals in them, too.

There's a new teacher in the school this year and I have him for English. *Him,* did you notice? He is *so* stunning, Sara. I know you always thought I was boy crazy but did you ever think

I'd be teacher crazy? Well, if you saw Mr. Hartley you'd understand. Mr. *D*. Hartley. I keep wondering what the *D* stands for.

Mary Lou and Cathanne and Patty are in the class and they have it bad, too. But *I* sit right up front. His eyes are like piercing blue flames. I wish I was thin so he'd like me.

D? Do you think it could stand for Dustin?

3

On Sunday afternoon it rained hard. But my mother and father went out anyway to the rummage sale and barn dance that one of my mother's clubs was holding. My mother belonged to lots of different organizations and was on all sorts of committees. I could tell my father hated to go, but she made him because she had "volunteered" him to take tickets and "count the house."

I was glad they were leaving because Mary Lou was coming over at two-thirty.

"Now be a good hostess, Glenda," my mother cautioned. "There are plenty of refreshments in the refrigerator and in the kitchen cupboard. Be sure to offer something to Mary Ann."

"Mary Lou," I corrected. "Only she's the one who hardly eats anything. And *I'm* certainly not planning to."

My mother made a clicking sound with her tongue.

"My, such will power. That Sara must be some kind of a magician, casting a no-eating spell on you from clear across the country."

My father was standing just outside the back door holding an open umbrella. "Come on, Grace," he called. "If we're going, let's go."

"Oh, that reminds me," my mother added. "It's raining pretty hard, so make sure your friend doesn't come in the front door. And see that she wipes her feet very carefully. I don't want the kitchen linoleum tracked up either."

Clutching Mr. Hartley's English anthology to my chest, I watched the car pull slowly out of the driveway and heaved a sigh of relief. I had found a poem I was going to use for my assignment. If Mary Lou wanted that one, it was "taken."

The poem was long and sort of old-fashioned. It was by Elizabeth Barrett Browning. Maybe she too had been fat, or maybe she'd been funny-looking or too old. It started out:

> *If thou must love me, let it be for naught*
> *Except for love's sake only. Do not say,*
> *"I love her for her smile—her look—her way*
> *Of speaking gently,—for a trick of thought*
> *That falls in well with mine . . ."*

and so on.

Of course, poetic words like "thou" and "naught" had to be translated into "you" and "nothing." Although the poem went on for fourteen lines, I felt I understood it pretty well and that I could explain it in my own words. It ended by saying:

... love me for love's sake, that evermore
Thou mayst love on, through love's eternity.

I thought the poem was really beautiful. I was mouthing it softly to myself, trying to understand some of the in-between lines better, when the front doorbell rang. I jumped up, slammed the book closed, and jammed it under my pillow—just a sort of nervous reaction, I guess.

Since Mary Lou had hardly ever been to my house and probably didn't even know where the back door was, I decided I'd just have to ignore my mother's warning about making her come in that way. It would be really embarrassing to send her around back in the rain.

As I peeked out the front window just to make sure who was there, I saw two figures standing on the stoop. They were giggling and squealing.

I flung open the door.

"Oh, my!" Mary Lou exclaimed, shaking the sides of her long yellow slicker. "Is it ever raining." She turned to the person standing alongside her. "It's lucky your father gave us a lift part way."

I looked at the other girl who was wearing a hooded jacket and floppy jeans with very wet bottoms. It was Patty, who sat in the back of the English class with Cathanne and Mary Lou. I was surprised to see her, but I nodded. "Hi," I said. "Come on in."

"I hope you don't mind I brought Patty along," Mary Lou panted. As they tiptoed across the living room carpet trying not to leave wet footprints, Mary Lou commented, "My, what a pretty house."

I led them part way down the hall and straight into

19

the den because I didn't want them to see my room with all the "get thin" pep poems from Sara tacked to the wall. Patty would be sure to tell Cathanne, and it would be all over school in no time.

Mary Lou looked around the den admiringly. "Everything's just so. Oh, I really do like your house, Glenda."

"Very nice, very nice," Patty murmured. She was short and slightly built but with a wide face and mouth, big dark eyes, and short thick brown hair.

"What's with Cathanne?" I asked, as they gave me their wet things to hang up in the bathroom. Cathanne and Patty had been almost inseparable all through sixth and seventh grade. Cathanne was much taller than Patty and had long red hair and a small pointed nose, but usually they did everything together and even talked in unison, as if they were one person.

"Cathanne has a *date* today," Mary Lou volunteered. "Would you believe it?"

"She's getting so uppity lately," Patty said, with a hurt look. "She wouldn't even tell me who it was. Me, her best friend. A ninth-grade boy was all she said. They were going to the roller rink."

"A date, huh?" I could just see Cathanne at the rink, skating gracefully, her long red hair flying. If I ever lost enough weight to have a figure like hers, let my hair grow long, and had it straightened . . .

"My mother says going-on-thirteen's too young to have a private date," Patty went on. "She says you should go out in a group but not one to one, if you know what I mean, till you're at least fourteen."

"Cathanne *looks* older, though," Mary Lou pointed out.

"I know," Patty said mournfully. "I'm so short I look

about eleven. If only I'd *grow*." She turned to me. "You lost a little weight this summer, didn't you, Glenda?"

I nodded and blushed.

"Yes, I thought so, too," Mary Lou chimed in. "What's your secret? Somebody told me they saw you jogging the other day in this royal-blue jogging suit with white bands."

"Who?" I asked sharply. "Who?"

"Goodness," Mary Lou said, "I can't remember. What's so important who it was?"

"Oh, you can't remember anything," I said disgustedly. "Was it Roddy Fenton?" I almost gagged just saying his name and thinking about that "Jelly Belly" remark.

"Gracious, no. At least I don't think so. Roddy's in a different home room this year, so I can't even recollect if I've talked to him lately."

"Oh," I said, falling into a chair with some relief. "So maybe he isn't the one."

"Which one?" Patty asked with a puzzled look on her face.

"Nothing, forget it. Listen, I'm supposed to ask you would anybody like some refreshments. My mother, you know. She's always worried people aren't getting enough to eat."

The moment I said that I was embarrassed, so I tried to make a joke of it. "Like me," I added, looking down at myself. "I'm the result."

Patty dropped her eyes. "Um, I'd like a Coke if you have it, Glenda. Or—or a diet soda, if that's all you have."

"Nothing for me," Mary Lou said. "I ate this enormous tuna fish plate for lunch. I think that's very heavy food smack in the middle of the day."

I started for the kitchen to get Patty her Coke. Then I stuck my head back in the den and said, "You're absolutely right, Mary Lou. You shouldn't have eaten the plate."

That broke them both up. When I came back in the den with Patty's Coke and a bowl of potato chips, Patty said, "You know, Glenda, you should start hanging out with us, with Mary Lou and me. We'd make a really good threesome. Two girls are too cliquey. Three are just right. Then, if one can't do something, the other two still have each other, and nobody gets stood up."

"You mean the way you'd get stood up if you were just two, and one had a date with a boy," Mary Lou suggested.

Patty nodded. "Yup. Right."

"Oh, I don't know," I said. "Two worked out pretty well when Sara and I were friends. We didn't have any big problems."

Mary Lou leaned forward. "That was last year, Glenda. We were all babies then. Things are getting more complicated now. This is eighth grade, for heaven's sake."

I couldn't help thinking how much Mary Lou and Patty sounded like my mother. And I suppose it was true that I ought to get some new friends. But I could just see the three of us hanging around school together—pale, skinny Mary Lou, short little Patty, and me, fat Glenda. What a freaky-looking threesome!

I leaned over and took a couple of potato chips from the bowl. Just a couple. "You're not ditching Cathanne," I said to Patty, "just because she has one single date with a boy, are you?"

"Oh, of course not," Patty said, wide-eyed. "I'm not ditching her at all. It's more like, well, like it's the other way around."

"Cathanne's so boy crazy," Mary Lou confided. "And she's getting so . . . brazen lately. She'll walk up to anybody and start flirting. You'll never guess what she did. She bought a tee shirt, a real tight one. It says on it: 'Come get me.' She says she's going to wear it to school next week!"

"And she's been getting so conceited lately," Patty added, a little out of breath. "She insists Mr. Hartley never takes his eyes off her. She says he has a 'thing' for her."

I gulped and reached for more potato chips. Crunch, munch, crunch. Good grief, I thought, what am I doing?

"Listen," I said, jumping up from the chair, "speaking of Mr. Hartley, let me go get my English book. That's what you came over for this afternoon. Right, Mary Lou? You still want me to help you pick out a poem?"

"Oh, definitely."

"Me, too," Patty murmured. "If you don't mind, that is."

I went hurrying off to my room, stuffing another bunch of potato chips into my mouth. All this talk about Cathanne and Mr. Hartley was making me very nervous.

I reached under the pillow where I'd stuck the English book with the poem I'd already secretly picked out for myself. Just as I was patting the pillow back

23

into place, I heard footsteps coming down the hall toward my room.

"Oh, my gracious!" a voice exclaimed right behind me. "Just *look* at Glenda's room. Come on here, Patty. It's real colorful."

I turned around red-faced. Mary Lou was standing just inside the doorway, her eyes darting around the walls from one square of brightly colored construction paper to another, reading Sara's verses, which were written on them in bold letters with a felt pen. Patty was already standing on tiptoe right behind her.

"Well, I never," Mary Lou squealed, as she began to rattle off some of the verses. Patty read a few along with her. "Imagine," Mary Lou said, "having all these warnings staring you in the face when you go to bed at night."

Patty giggled. "She can't see them at *night*, stupid." They both seemed to have forgotten me completely.

Mary Lou tapped Patty on the shoulder. "You know who these'd be good for?" Mary Lou remarked. "Robert, fat Robert."

Patty laughed even harder. "Oh, yeah, I know who you mean. Glenda ought to invite him over to see her room."

"He is so fat, I can't *stand* him," Mary Lou exclaimed. "Ooh, it's just disgustin' the way he shakes all over." Mary Lou stopped short and looked at me apologetically. "Oh, he's much fatter than you, Glenda. He is really fat."

"I don't even know who you're talking about," I said coldly.

"Of course, you do," Mary Lou retorted. "He sits

about halfway back in the English room. Robert Fry, that's his name. Fat Robert Fry."

I shook my head and brushed some hair out of my eyes. "I never even noticed him," I protested, still feeling very uncomfortable at all the awful things these people who wanted to be my friends were saying about fat people. Sara would never have acted like that.

"Never *noticed* him!" Patty sputtered. "That would be like not noticing if an elephant walked into the English class." Her eyes kept right on roving the walls of my room, as she giggled at Sara's poems one after the other.

"Oh, look, look!" she exploded, grabbing Mary Lou's sleeve. "Look at that one." She pointed to a candy-pink poster printed in thick chocolate-brown letters. The next moment, with tears practically running down her cheeks and holding her stomach to try to keep from laughing even harder, she read the poem out loud:

> *Eating hot fudge sundaes*
> *In your dreams*
> *Means you won't have to let out*
> *Any more seams!*

4

The rest of the day was just terrible. I made Mary Lou and Patty go home early because I said I had a headache and wouldn't be able to help them pick a poem for English.

I could see they were both sort of sorry because they kept looking back at me with big sad eyes, especially Patty, as I practically pushed them out the door into the rain. It wasn't raining that hard by then, but I wouldn't have cared if it had been coming down in sheets.

Then I went back to the den and turned on the TV and had a Coke and finished the whole bowl of potato chips. I knew what I was doing, but I just didn't care.

What was the use anyway? I'd been suffering all summer, starving myself, and still ashamed to go to the beach where any of the kids from school might see me. I'd managed to lose sixteen whole pounds, and *still* somebody had called me "Jelly Belly." And now Mary Lou and Patty, without exactly wanting to be mean, had shown me what people really thought of you if you were fat.

On top of all that my mother came home all excited because Miss Esme had come to the rummage sale and barn dance where she'd distributed her brand new leaflets about the dancercises and slimnastics and all the other classes she was going to be starting soon.

My mother handed me a leaflet with a picture of Miss Esme on it. She was dark-haired and long-faced, and wearing a black leotard that showed the outlines of her *bones*. She did have bulging muscles on her legs but not an ounce of fat anywhere.

"And just listen to what Miss Esme said, Glenda," my mother reported bouncily. "I told her that you were into jogging and seemed to want to keep on doing that. And she said, 'No problem. I'm going to have outdoor jogging classes as part of the program. Glenda can concentrate on whatever aspect she enjoys most.' Now isn't that nice?"

"No," I said grumpily, handing back the leaflet. "I don't want to go running through the streets with a lot of other fat people."

"Glenda, you're *not* fat," my mother scolded. "I wish you wouldn't think of yourself that way. Chubby, maybe. Still padded from your little girl days. But that's all it is. A little of the right kind of exercise, some bending and stretching, a sensible diet, and it would all just melt away."

"That's not true!" I shot back. "I *am* fat. Everybody

27

says so. Nothing I ever do will make me thin. And you know who's fault it is? Yours. *Your* fault."

My mother spread a plump hand across her chest. Rings glittered on three of her dimpled fingers. *"My* fault? Why, baby, how can you say that? What did *I* do?"

"Don't you *see?"* I answered impatiently. "It's because you're a fat person, too. Only you won't admit it. You wear a tight girdle and an uplift bra and . . . and you're older. *Your* friends don't make fun of you. But I inherited all my fatness from you." I tore my fingers through my hair. "O-o-h, why couldn't I have been born to somebody skinny? Like . . . like Sara's mother."

Just then my father walked into the den with his newspaper in his hand.

"Can anybody tell me what all the screaming's about?" he wanted to know. "It sounds like hens fighting in a barnyard. Haven't I already heard enough noise for one day?"

"Harold," my mother said, almost tearfully. "I wish you'd talk to your daughter. She says *I'm* the reason she's fat. After all I've tried to do to help her. But will she listen to me? No. She'd rather take the advice of some kooky family that used to live up the street!"

With that, she stamped out of the room.

My father sat down on the den couch and patted a place for me beside him. I sat down sulkily.

"Now, listen," he said, patting my hand gently. "Why all this rumpus all of a sudden? You're doing fine. Umpteen pounds off this summer. How many was it you lost?"

I shook my head miserably. "She shouldn't talk about Sara's family like that. I know she never liked them, but Sara's the best friend I ever . . . h-had."

I began to sob. My father patted my hand harder and faster. He looked helpless, his graying moustache twitching a little and the light glinting off his glasses. He had a round pale face and he was also beginning to have a round belly that stuck out in front of him when he walked.

"Well," he said, clearing his throat, "I guess jogging the way you've been doing is okay. A lot of the fellows at the office do it. But maybe your mother would feel better if you took her advice once in a while. I met that Esme woman at the barn dance this afternoon. She seems to have a kind face. And she's *very* skinny."

I looked down at my father's hand, still resting on mine but patting more slowly now. "I'm not going jogging anymore," I said in a small voice, "alone or with anybody. And as far as going in for any other exercises, I'd probably just end up eating more. The way *she* does."

"If you mean your mother, then say so, Glenda," my father remarked. "Don't call her 'she'."

I choked back a heavy sob. "And . . . and look what I did this afternoon," I went on. I pointed to the empty potato-chip bowl that was still sitting on the low table in front of the couch.

My father followed my glance with a puzzled look. *"That,"* I said, impatiently, lifting my foot and giving the bowl a kick. "I . . . I got upset about something that happened. And the next thing I knew . . ."

29

Suddenly there was a short, high-pitched screech from the living room. A moment later my mother came rushing into the den.

"Glenda," she said accusingly, "did you let that girl in the front door? You did, didn't you?"

I looked up at her defiantly. "I let both of them in."

"Both!" my mother shrilled. "There were two of them? No wonder there are so many foot marks. I'm going to have to have that whole rug shampooed. Oh, Glenda," she wrung her hands, "what am I going to do with you?"

My father pointed a finger at her. "I told you not to get oyster-white carpeting for the front of the house, Grace. You have a fit over every footstep anyone takes in there."

"It's not oyster," my mother snapped back. "It's clamshell. And I'll thank you, Harold, to stay out of it. This is between Glenda and me."

I scrambled to my feet. "You told me I should have friends," I shrieked at my mother. "You said I should be nice to them. What do you want me to d-o-o-o!"

"Glenda," my mother stormed back, "don't you dare shout at me in that hysterical tone of voice." She pursed her lips trying to get control of herself. "Go to your room, Glenda. Go to your room this minute."

I brushed past her in a frenzy.

"I'm going," I said. "And I'm never coming out. Never!"

Mr. Hartley's blue eyes met mine.

"Glenda Waite, is that right?"

I managed to whisper, "Yes."

A little more than a week had gone by since my big fight with my mother. I was still grouchy and sulky around the house, and she was tight-lipped and cross-looking with me. The only good thing was that all of her committees were getting very busy with their fall meetings and she wasn't home as much as before.

It was also about a week since we'd handed in our love poem assignments to English class. Each day I'd sat in my front row seat looking up with more and more adoring eyes at Mr. D. Hartley. And each day I'd felt like I was sitting at the base of a magnificent statue or watching some thrilling image on a twenty-foot-tall movie screen. I knew *he* was there, but he didn't seem to have any idea *I* was.

Now, for the very first time, Mr. Hartley had actually said my name and looked deep into my eyes. If that was the way he'd been looking at Cathanne, no wonder she'd been acting so crazy and actually believing her English teacher was in love with her.

"Well, Glenda Waite, I've got a job for you," Mr. Hartley said in his magical deep-soft voice. "Come on up here and get these poetry assignments." He indicated the pile of papers on his desk that we had all handed in. "There's a short list of students' names on top. I'd like you to take the whole batch back to your seat and pick out just the papers belonging to each of those students. Then give them back their papers. They're the ones who made outstanding poetry choices that we're going to be talking about in class today."

I wriggled out from behind my desk as gracefully

as I could. I knew my face was red because my cheeks felt fiery. As I walked the short distance to Mr. Hartley's desk, I could really feel those extra three pounds I'd put back on this past week. Disregarding all of Sara's warnings and advice, I'd been eating snacks out of the refrigerator, drinking sodas (not even diet), and munching on anything that crunched or crackled, or that I could otherwise gnash my teeth on. And, as I'd told my father I was going to, I'd quit jogging. Worst of all, I hadn't even *walked* to the mailbox because I hadn't written Sara a letter in over a week.

What was the use? Everything I did made me a laughing stock. So I might as well stay as I was, get fatter. Who cared?

Mr. Hartley was at the blackboard now, talking to the class about the regular lesson for the day. I prayed he'd turn to write on the board as I got closer or keep looking past me at Mary Lou and Cathanne and Patty in the back of the room. Why couldn't I move faster, get the papers more quickly, and scramble back to my desk before Mr. Hartley got a good look at me standing up? Everything seemed to be happening in slow motion. And just as I reached for the pile of papers, Mr. Hartley stopped talking to the class altogether.

He lunged forward and his hand almost brushed mine as he nudged the papers toward me. "That's it, Glenda," he said. "Just find the ones that belong to the seven names on the list. Afraid I got the assignments all mixed up after I read them." His eyes met mine again. They were twinkling and there was a teasing smile on his lips.

I nodded and dashed back clumsily to the safety of my desk. I didn't really care what the rest of the class must be thinking about how fat I looked. After all, I was used to kids making fun of me all my life. All I cared about was what Mr. Hartley was thinking.

While Mr. Hartley went on talking about the lesson, I began to read silently down the list of names. Alice Mackenzie, a small, eager girl with glasses who sat across the aisle from me, leaned over to try to see the list. "Want me to help?" she whispered.

I shook my head no and pulled the list closer where she couldn't see it.

I ran my eye down it quickly. Of all things, Robert Fry's name was on the list. Fat Robert Fry. I knew who he was by now. I guess I'd even known who he was when Mary Lou had mentioned his name at my house that rainy Sunday. I just didn't *want* to notice him, I suppose. He had a friendly, sincere face. And he *was* fatter than I was. But that didn't make me feel any better. People sometimes think fat people might want to hang around with other fat people. But who needs to call extra attention to themselves? Of course, if they're with skinny people, they also stand out. Like I said before, there's no way to win, so why bother?

Alice Mackenzie was practically falling out of her seat trying to read the list even though I'd moved it pretty far away.

"Hey," she whispered again, "I'm not on it. And I picked such a good poem. But," she added in a disappointed voice, *"you* are. What poem did you pick, Glenda?"

Alice had a quick eye all right. There, near the bottom of the page, in Mr. Hartley's sharp, slanting handwriting, my own name was scrawled: Glenda Waite.

I stared blankly at Alice. All I could think of in that instant was that Robert Fry and I were on the same list. And in a flash (even though I knew it couldn't really be true), the thought crossed my mind that maybe this wasn't simply a list of the kids who'd done a good job on the poetry assignment; it was a list of the fattest people in the class!

5

"So," I concluded, standing up in the front of the English room and reading from the paper I'd written, "I picked this poem because I think it says a very important thing. It says that you should love someone not for what they look like, or for how they speak or act, or because you pity them. Those are all things that can change as time goes on. You should love them for love itself, because true love will prove itself by going on and on forever."

I lowered my eyes. My hands were shaking. I was wet with perspiration. Even the roots of my hair felt damp. And my fingerprints had left dimpled circles on the page I'd been reading from.

The classroom was awfully quiet. I'd been the first person Mr. Hartley had called on to get up and tell about the poem they'd picked.

"Any comments? Questions?" Mr. Hartley looked around the room.

Nobody said anything. A few people squirmed in their seats and grinned slyly at the person sitting alongside. I glanced up and caught Patty's wide-eyed stare and Mary Lou's blank one. Oh, why didn't *they* say anything. They had said they wanted to be my friends. Anything just to break this deadly silence.

All of a sudden a hand shot up from somewhere in the middle of the room. Mr. Hartley said, "Yes, Robert?"

I realized the hand belonged to Robert Fry. Fat Robert Fry.

With a lot of creaking and straining noises from the furniture, Robert got up from his desk and rose to his full height. He was pretty tall as well as fat.

His smooth face was almost expressionless as he spoke, and his dark hair lay neat and shining across his brow.

"I think it's very interesting," he began, clearing his throat a couple of times, "that she . . . um, Glenda . . . chose a poem about loving another person. After all, the assignment said a 'love poem,' but it didn't say what kind. I mean, it could have been a poem about love of country, love of nature, love of the sea, anything like that."

Mr. Hartley snapped his fingers. "Excellent point, Robert. How many people picked a poem that *didn't* deal with romantic love between men and women?"

Only a few hands went up and there were snickers. Cathanne rolled her eyes and sighed. "What else is there?" Somebody else made kissing sounds.

Mr. Hartley motioned for the class to calm down.

"Oh," Robert continued, still standing at his seat, "I didn't mean there was anything wrong with a . . . romantic love poem. In fact, I myself chose a poem very similar to the one that Glenda did. It's . . . well, almost a twin to hers."

"That's right," said Mr. Hartley, nodding. "When I read it, I thought the similarity was very striking." He gave me one of his glittering blue-eyed looks and a dazzling half-smile. "You two didn't happen to work on the assignment together, did you?"

I began to get red-faced and shook my head vigorously from side to side.

"No, I guess not," Mr. Hartley said quickly. "Although there'd certainly be nothing wrong if you had."

Nothing wrong! Did Mr. Hartley, too, see Robert and me as two fatties and therefore a perfect pair? My expression must have shown how outraged I felt at the very idea.

Mr. Hartley gave me a surprised little glance and said in a soft voice, "Why don't you take your seat now, Glenda? We'll have Robert read his poem, and then we'll discuss both poems and compare them. Okay?"

He sounded coaxing and even a little apologetic. I sat down at my desk, relieved to get out of the limelight for a while. I was feeling even more embarrassed now than when I'd finished my report.

At Robert's desk there was more squeaking and creaking and the sound of rustling papers.

"Um, I think I'll come up front and read it, okay?" Robert suggested.

"By all means," Mr. Hartley said, stepping aside and making room for Robert.

Robert approached with heavy steps and planted himself directly in front of my desk. Even after he stopped walking, the blubbery fat on his body just kept on shaking. You could see it trying to settle down right through his shirt.

I couldn't resist turning around to take a peek at Mary Lou. Sure enough, her face was turned sideways toward Patty, and her hand was covering her mouth, cheek, and eye. I couldn't tell if she was talking or laughing or just being nauseated because she found Robert so "disgustin'."

Robert cleared his throat. "This poem," he began, "is by 'anonymous.' That means that nobody knows who wrote it."

A couple of kids laughed. Were they laughing at the word *anonymous* or at fat Robert himself?

He went on unperturbed. "Okay, here's how it starts." Some more throat-clearing, and then he read, carefully emphasizing all the words that rhymed:

> *Love me not for comely grace,*
> *For my pleasing eye or face,*
> *Nor for any outward part,*
> *No, nor for my constant heart,*

At this point Robert stopped reading for a moment and looked around the room as if to say, "Everybody got that so far?"

Then, giving us all another searching glance, he went on:

For those may fail, or turn to ill,
So thou and I shall sever:

Again Robert looked up. This time his eye fell directly on me.

Keep therefore a true woman's eye
And love me still, but know not why—
So hast thou the same reason still
To dote upon me ever!

The poem was finished, I guess. But it remained very quiet in the classroom.

Maybe some people were trying to figure out what it meant. But I didn't have any trouble with that. I understood Robert's poem all too well. Somebody fat or ugly or weird-looking was begging somebody else to ignore what they saw on the outside and to love them only for themselves.

I didn't dare look up, just in case Robert was still looking at me in that same meaningful way. Our poems *were* alike. He was right about that. And now I was going to have to sit there listening to the class talk about how come, by some strange coincidence, Robert and I had chosen poems that said the same thing.

I knew how come, and it wasn't a coincidence. Fat Robert and Fat Glenda had picked similar poems because—on the outside anyway—*they* were alike!

That evening I wrote a long letter to Sara.

Sara, I've been awful—eating fattening junk and not jogging anymore, and I gained three pounds in one week! Well, it all started when somebody called me "Jelly Belly." I keep thinking it might have been Roddy Fenton. But I have no proof.

Now there's this terribly fat boy in my English class. He's very intelligent and all that, but he is gross. What's even worse, I think he sort of likes me. After English class today he hung around and wanted to talk to me. I think he thinks we have a lot in common.

Well, I don't want to have a lot in common with him. Just because he and I look similar on the outside (although he is *much* fatter than I am) doesn't mean we're the same on the inside.

So I'm thinking I just *have* to change the outside. Otherwise how will anybody know that I'm different inside and I'm not a twin for fat Robert. Oh, that's his name—fat Robert Fry. Well, really Robert Fry. But you know how kids talk.

Sara, remember your poem about the *thin* me inside that will someday get out? Well, if it kills me I'm going to take off another sixteen pounds by Thanksgiving. And then another sixteen by Valentine's Day. And so on. How can I go on looking this way in front of Mr. Hartley? You remember him—my English teacher.

Sara, he actually spoke to me privately today for a little while after class (while fat Robert was waiting over near the door). It was about a report I gave that he thought was very good. And for that little while I had the feeling of what it must be like to be really beautiful and *thin* all over!

Oh, he's sensational, Sara! And imagine, I still don't even know his first name. Neither does anybody else. If it were Derek that would be nice, wouldn't it?

6

My mother actually threw her arms around me and squeezed me hard.

"Oh, Glenda, you've made me *so* happy. I'll call Miss Esme right now and tell her you'll take the four o'clock dancercise class on Tuesdays and Thursdays and join the Saturday morning jogging group."

"Now wait a minute," I said, edging away from her slowly loosening grip. "I didn't *say* that. I just said I'd go next Tuesday and watch. I have to see if I like it first."

My mother shook her head. "What good is watching? How can you tell if you like it if you don't actually try it?"

I looked away. "I don't know. I just don't think you should spend all that money before I . . ."

"Nonsense. What do you think Miss Esme is, some sort of an ogre? She isn't going to insist on full payment at the very first lesson. Besides, remember the discount she promised. Oh, Glenda, couldn't you at least try to talk some of your friends into taking the class with you?"

"Who?" I asked, thrusting out my hands in exasperation. "Sara would. But she'd need a private jet to get here and back home three times a week."

My mother examined some chipped polish on her thumbnail. "Well, what about those two girls who were here that Sunday and left those awful dirty tracks on my new living-room carpet. They owe me that at least. Rug shampooing gets more expensive all the time."

I groaned. "Can't you just see me telling them *that?*"

"Oh, come on, baby." My mother smiled faintly. "There are all *sorts* of ways of approaching people. Try, Glenda dear. And I'll tell Miss Esme we're getting a little group together. I'm sure she'll make a reduction in the price."

I was glad I'd picked breakfast time on a school day to tell my mother I was considering Miss Esme's classes after all. At least our discussion about it had to come to an end before we got into another fight.

As I left the house, I tucked the letter to Sara into one of my school books. I would drop it in the very first mailbox I came to. Once the letter with my promises to Sara was on its way, I'd be pretty sure not to back out.

The first thing I saw when I got to the schoolyard was a big bunch of kids standing around in a circle, watching something that was going on in the middle. A fight probably. I walked up to the outer fringe of the crowd. I didn't like to get too close. Sometimes the kids

43

who were fighting would get real rough and a whole bunch of onlookers would start edging away in a backward stampede. It was very easy to get knocked down and even stepped on.

But this time things seemed pretty quiet. Maybe it was a wrestling match, somebody holding somebody else down and just a lot of heavy breathing. I moved in a little closer and tried to poke my head between two other heads.

"Hey, what's going on?"

One of the heads swung around. It was Roddy Fenton. I gasped.

I hadn't seen him all summer, and he wasn't in any of my eighth-grade classes this year. Up close I could see he'd changed a little and he'd also gotten taller. But he still had that teasing expression and that stiff way of turning his head on his long skinny neck.

"Oh, hi, Glenda." His voice had gotten deeper, too. "How've you been?"

"Okay," I said softly. "How about you?"

He was being very civil for Roddy, who used to call me "Fat" and tell everybody I was a squealer because I had actually seen Roddy's older brother—who went around with a bad crowd for a while—steal a neighbor's car. And I'd reported it to the police because my mother said we had to. The way Roddy acted toward me after that, I realized I'd probably made an enemy for life. But what else could I have done?

Roddy actually moved aside and gave me his place so I could peek into the center of the circle. "Take a look," he said.

I still didn't trust him. Why couldn't he first say what was happening?

44

I craned my neck and finally managed to catch a glimpse of what was going on. There, in the middle of the crowd, wearing only a tight tee shirt and a pair of skinny jeans, even though the morning was cool and brisk, was Cathanne. She was snapping her fingers and tossing her head and doing a kind of combination tap-and-jazz dance routine. There was no music, but some kids standing near her were moving their shoulders to the same rhythm.

"Wow," I said to Roddy, after watching carefully for a while. "She's pretty good. How come, though?"

Roddy shrugged. "She thinks she's auditioning for a Broadway show. I don't know." His voice had suddenly broken into a high squeak. "Probably just showing off."

"Glenda!" Somebody poked my shoulder hard. I wheeled around. It was Patty, closely followed by Mary Lou. Out of the corner of my eye I saw Roddy slowly walk off without saying anything else.

"What's up with Cathanne?" I demanded. "Roddy says she's going to be in a Broadway show."

"She is," Patty replied, breathing hard. "That is, if Mr. Hartley gives her a part."

I opened my mouth in astonishment. "Mr. Hartley? What's he got to do with . . ."

"Oh, didn't you hear?" Mary Lou gushed. "Mr. Hartley's going to direct the school play this year. Only it isn't going to be a play; it's going to be a musical revue. Just like on Broadway."

"That's right," Patty chimed in. "It's going to have songs, dances, skits, magic acts, all kinds of specialty numbers. But mostly lots of singing and dancing. Oh, I hope I can get into it, but I just bet all the best parts go to ninth-graders."

"And to Cathanne," Mary Lou reminded her.

"And to Cathanne," Patty repeated, casting a glance toward the kids who were still watching Cathanne's dance routine. "Of course, *I* don't do that kind of dancing," Patty remarked firmly. "It's all formula stuff. It doesn't have any natural expression. I prefer modern dance, free-form body movement." She looked at me intently. "Know what I mean?"

I nodded blankly. I was still in a state of shock about Mr. Hartley directing the school musical revue. "How . . . how did you find out he . . . Mr. Hartley . . ."

"Oh, that," Mary Lou replied. *"She* found out. Cathanne. She hangs around him a lot. Yesterday she actually walked to his car with him after school."

"He didn't give her a lift home, though," Patty said quickly. "She told me herself he didn't. That's a rumor. Though, secretly, I think she's the one who started it!" Patty giggled uncomfortably.

"Course not," Mary Lou added. "He doesn't even live here in town. And anyhow he wouldn't do a dumb thing like that. It could get him in trouble."

"Especially with *her*." Patty rolled her eyes.

Cathanne must have quit dancing now, because the crowd was breaking up and just a few kids remained clustered in a tight huddle around her. Patty and Mary Lou and I began to walk slowly toward the school building.

"It's strange," I mused, "about Mr. Hartley. Being an English teacher, I'd have thought he would want to direct a play with speaking parts."

"Yes, but you can get a lot more kids into the cast if you do a musical," Patty pointed out. "Almost anybody can do *something,* singing or dancing or being in a skit maybe."

"What can you do, Glenda?" Mary Lou asked. "Can you sing?"

My cheeks reddened. Actually I preferred dancing. Sometimes in my room, in front of my full-length mirror, I'd dance to some of my records or tapes. I didn't really know any steps. I'd just follow the music, doing any old thing that fit the rhythm. It felt good and it didn't look too bad either. At least to me, it didn't. But I was sure I wouldn't have the nerve to do it in front of anybody until I became a whole lot thinner.

"I'm better at dancing," I told Mary Lou almost defiantly. Why did most people think that all fat people had good voices but were terrible dancers?

Mary Lou looked at me a little surprised.

"I'm starting classes, in fact," I added in a sudden burst. "I'm taking dancercises. They're a sort of combination of all different styles of dancing *with* exercise. Get it?"

"You *are!*" Patty squealed, before Mary Lou could say anything. "Where?"

"Right here in t . . . t . . . town," I stammered. I couldn't understand why Patty was getting so excited.

"Where in town?" she demanded.

"At Miss Esme's studio. She's . . ."

"Oh, my goodness!" Patty shrieked, jumping up and down. "Starting on Tuesday? At four o'clock? The teen class?"

Now I was getting excited. "You too? Honestly?"

"Honestly," Patty said, crossing her heart. "What a coincidence. Isn't this great? I didn't think I'd know anybody in the class. Now we'll have each other. I told you, Glenda, that we should start hanging around together."

Mary Lou gave us both a sour look. "You know what *I* think? I think you two are kind of mean." She eyed Patty. "You never even told me about it. You could have said something."

"But I only got my father to agree to it yesterday," Patty said defensively. "I'm not even officially signed up yet."

"And I only decided last night," I protested. "My mother said she was going to call Miss Esme this morning to tell her okay. Listen," I added, "why don't you join up, too, Mary Lou? My mother says she can get us a discount if we have a little group. Really."

Patty began to urge her, too. "You'd like it, Mary Lou. And then we'd be a threesome. And, listen, maybe Miss Esme could even help us work out our own dance routine for the show. Wouldn't that be something?"

Mary Lou looked doubtful. "I don't know. It sounds like it could be awfully strenuous. And I do hate sweating. Ugh. Feeling all wet and sticky. And the smell of perspiration. It's . . . disgustin'."

Patty and I looked at each other and burst out laughing.

Mary Lou looked hurt. "I don't see what's so funny." She tucked her books more tightly into her arms. "You can try as you may, but neither of you will ever come close to dancing as well as Cathanne. She's going to be the star of the show and you know it."

"Who's trying to be the star?" Patty questioned.

But Mary Lou wasn't answering. She was already walking away toward the homeroom.

Patty clasped my wrist. "Listen, Glenda, I'm really glad you and I are going to be in the dancercise class together. It'll be fun."

I felt good about it, too.

"I also hope it'll help me to lose a little weight," I confided.

Even though Patty had made fun of Sara's verses tacked up in my room, I could tell that she'd been sorry later. So, with a grin, I recited one of the very short ones for her:

> *Thin is happy,*
> *Fat is sappy.*

Then we both laughed.

7

Talk about fat, there was Robert Fry standing just outside the English room a few days later, before the period began. He seemed to be waiting for someone.

"Hi," he said with a broad smile as I came walking down the hall with Patty. He hadn't been in class for a while, much to my relief.

Patty gave me a quick sideways glance as we entered the room. Robert followed closely and planted himself at my desk.

"I've been absent," he said, looking at me with a very serious expression. "Had some trouble with my foot. Wonder if you could give me the homework assignment, Glenda, and any class notes that I missed."

Patty smothered a giggle and glided away toward the back of the room. "Traitor," I muttered under my breath.

I sat down clumsily at my desk. "Well, um, let's see . . ." I couldn't seem to find my notebook. Why did

Robert have to pick on me? It was so embarrassing. Any minute now Mr. Hartley would walk into the room and see the two fatties with their heads together.

To make matters worse, Robert had squeezed himself into Alice Mackenzie's seat, directly across the aisle from me, and leaned his mountainous body over toward my desk. My fingers tore through the pages.

"You know what," I said. "I think I left my assignment book home today. And the notes, I just can't find them."

Robert poked a thick finger at one of the pages. "No," I said quickly. "That's history. Why don't you ask Mr. Hartley? Or one of the other kids?"

Robert uttered a deep sigh and stood up. "Sure," he said. "I'll get it from somebody else. Sorry I bothered you."

Instantly I felt sorry. What was I doing? I was treating Robert the same way lots of people had treated me, people who just didn't want to have anything to do with a fat person. If only Robert's fatness didn't make *me* so self-conscious. . . .

"Um . . . how's your foot now?" I inquired, as Robert began to walk away. I felt I just had to say something.

He seemed to brighten instantly.

"It's fine," he said, lifting it up and shaking it as if to assure me. "Actually it wasn't my foot, it was my toe. Ingrown toenail. Ever have one of those?"

I made a face. "I've heard they're awful."

"Yup. It hurt a lot. They had to cut real deep into the nail, and I had to keep soaking it in a wet dressing. Couldn't get a shoe on."

"I'm . . . sorry," I said, looking up at him. "I really am."

He smiled bravely, cheerfully. Actually Robert had a very nice smile. I wondered what he'd look like thin. But I couldn't imagine it, no matter how hard I tried.

As soon as the English class ended, Cathanne raced up to the front of the room and started talking earnestly to Mr. Hartley in a corner over near the window. I couldn't hear what she was saying, but I took a guess it had something to do with the show. A moment later Mary Lou joined her. Ever since she'd gotten annoyed with Patty and me, I noticed she'd been hanging around Cathanne like a pale shadow.

Somebody poked me on the shoulder. It was Patty. "Hey," she said urgently, "stop fiddling with your books and come on over to Mr. Hartley with me. I want to hear what she's saying to him. It's a free country."

I felt funny about doing that because it seemed nosy, but I got out of my seat and obediently followed Patty.

Cathanne was wearing the tight tee shirt she'd danced in in the schoolyard a few days before. Her long red hair was thick and silky, and I noticed she had some green eye shadow on her lids. She had changed a lot since the days when we were in sixth and seventh grade together. Her small pointed nose seemed more upturned and her lips were fuller and prettier.

"I can do any dance, *any*," she was saying breathlessly to Mr. Hartley. "Just give me an idea what you're looking for and I'll work up a routine for the auditions."

Patty exchanged a knowing glance with me. Mary

Lou kept her eyes fixed on Cathanne. Mr. Hartley smiled his teasing blue-eyed smile. "What can I say?" he remarked, looking around at all four of us. "I'm surrounded by eager, talented, and beauteous young women."

Patty pushed herself forward right next to where Cathanne was standing. "When *are* the auditions, Mr. Hartley? We'd all like to know so we could try out," she said in a sweetly innocent voice.

"A very good question," Mr. Hartley answered with an exaggerated shrug. "I'm trying to clear time in the gym and in the auditorium. But auditions are four, five weeks off at the very least. So," he looked at Cathanne, "I suggest we all take it easy for the time being. The show hasn't even been announced yet. I'm glad we're getting such enthusiastic response based on word of mouth. But . . ." he held up his hands, "no casting call yet."

"Couldn't you give us just a tiny little hint, though," Mary Lou asked softly, "as to what *kind* of show it's going to be?"

Mr. Hartley extended his arms as if to embrace all of us. "Mary Lou, Cathanne, Patty, Glenda," he said in a warm voice, "it's going to be the kind of show *you* make it. Actually, I'm a lazy guy and a lazy director. I'm not going to coach anyone in a big way. I'm going to use *your* talent, organize it and present it. You come to me, show me what you can do, and if it's stage material, you're in. Got that?"

We all nodded.

Mr. Hartley glanced at his watch. "Listen, you're all going to be late for your next class. Just remember, though. I want *everybody* to try out. That means you, too, Mary Lou. And you, Patty." He turned to me. "And you, Glenda. Will I see you at auditions?"

His eyes caught mine and held them. Blue flames shot through me. I gulped hard. "Yes," I answered recklessly.

"Bend . . . stretch . . . kick . . . kick. And *turn* . . . stretch . . . kick . . . kick. *Left* . . . stretch . . . kick . . . kick. And *right* . . . twist . . . *left* twist . . ."

A week had gone by. I'd already gone to two of Miss Esme's dancercise classes and jogged once with her Saturday morning group.

The first dancercise class hadn't been bad at all. The steps and the movements were easy, and the music was nice and zingy. I felt almost as good as when I put on one of my records and danced in front of my full-length mirror.

There were about fifteen people in the class and most of them were a funny shape, especially in their skin-tight leotards, so I didn't feel too self-conscious either. Even Miss Esme didn't have a beautiful figure. From her shoulders to her hips she was skinny all over. Then her thigh muscles and calf muscles bulged out in big bumps. And her feet turned outward like a ballet dancer's when she walked.

Today at our third session Miss Esme was giving us the steps for a new dancercise. But, oh, how much harder everything was getting. My body ached all over. I'd discovered muscles where I never knew I had any, in my shoulders and the backs of my thighs, in my buttocks and even in my wrists.

The strain was killing me. I was puffing like a steam engine.

"Okay," Miss Esme announced. "Break time. Ten minutes. Then we'll try it with the music."

I fell down on the floor in a quivering heap.

"What's wrong?" Patty asked. "You look all in."

"I . . . can't," I gasped. "Everything hurts so much."

Patty sat down on the floor beside me, hugging her knees. "That's because you're not in condition. Didn't you ever do any body movement before?"

I shook my head. "I guess not. I *thought* I did, running and all that. But this is . . . different."

"You should ask Miss Esme what to do. I'll get her."

"N . . . no," I started to say. But it was too late. Patty had dashed off.

A couple of minutes later she was back with Miss Esme. I scrambled into a sitting position. There was something about Miss Esme—her long mournful face, her serious eyes, her straight dark hair pulled severely back—that made me feel stiff and shy with her. She wasn't tough or bossy, but she never smiled either.

Miss Esme sat down crosslegged on the floor beside me.

"How are we doing?"

"Oh, fine," I said. "It's just . . ."

Miss Esme nodded. "Don't try to complete all the movements. Stretch only as far as you can go without feeling too much pain. You'll use up plenty of energy even if you just *sketch* in the exercises for a while. Easy does it." She put her hand on my arm. "Okay?"

"Un hmmm." I was beginning to really like her. Close up, I noticed for the first time that there were long threads of gray in her jet black hair. She was older than I'd thought, thirty-eight, maybe even forty.

"I suppose if I were thinner," I murmured, "it would be easier."

Miss Esme patted my wrist. She didn't say anything.

"She's nice," I said to Patty after Miss Esme was out of hearing. "At first I didn't want you to call her over. I'm so klutzy and dumb. I feel ashamed."

"Oh, come on," Patty said encouragingly. "You'll get there, Glenda."

"Yes, but *when?* I haven't got that much time."

Patty looked puzzled.

"The auditions," I said. "I want to try out for a part in the show. It's only a few weeks away. You heard what Mr. Hartley said."

"Sure. I know. But I didn't know *you* were going to try out."

"I am," I said. "I made up my mind. Didn't you even hear him ask me to? Listen, I'm not such a bad dancer. I have a pretty good sense of rhythm and I can learn steps real fast. It's just my . . . my . . . ." I punched myself in the belly. "But the way I'm starving myself, I've just *got* to start losing weight soon. Only I don't know if it'll be soon enough," I moaned.

Patty leaned forward. "Listen, Glenda, I'm your friend, so I'm telling you. Don't get your hopes up. I'm not saying you *won't* get a dancing part in the show. But what if you don't? Even *I* might not."

Patty's words really stabbed me. So she thought she was better than I was. Well, we'd see about that. I'd watched her in the dancercise class and I didn't think she was that great, only thinner.

Miss Esme clapped her hands together for attention. "On your feet, people."

I heaved myself up, actually forcing myself to enjoy

the pain of moving. I'd do the dance exercises if they killed me, jog every minute I could spare, live on tomatoes and lemons and ice water.

I'd get thin enough by audition time to dance for Mr. Hartley and to look good doing it. I'd show Patty, Mary Lou, Miss Esme, my mother, whoever had called me "Jelly Belly," all of them!

Sara had already gotten the letter I'd sent her resolving to lose sixteen pounds by Thanksgiving, in which I'd told her how I felt about Mr. Hartley. And she'd written back and said that she'd thought it all over and probably my big crush on Mr. Hartley was exactly the motivation I needed to get really thin.

In fact, she'd even written me a poem about it:

> To Glenda—
> *I can see you getting thinner,*
> > *partly*
> *To win the heart of*
> > *Mr. Hartley.*

I wasn't going to tack *that* one up on the wall.

8

Ever since Patty had found out that I was serious about trying out for Mr. Hartley's show, I noticed that she'd been acting cooler toward me. In one way that made me feel bad. But in another way I felt good. Maybe Patty secretly believed I stood a pretty good chance of getting into the show. Maybe she really was worried that Mr. Hartley would pick me at the audition and leave her out.

I decided not to say anything more to her about the tryouts. But if Patty wanted some good-natured, lumbering elephant for a friend, let her go to the zoo and find one. That wasn't going to be me. My muscles didn't ache nearly so much anymore. I jogged almost every day now, including Saturday, and even my mother didn't complain because she knew Miss Esme was in favor of jogging.

Patty wasn't in Miss Esme's Saturday morning running group. There were eight of us, and not all fat either. A few, in fact, were downright skinny. I was the youngest. All of the other joggers were grown-up women who didn't like to go running alone.

Miss Esme had a good route picked out that didn't go through a part of town where people or traffic would get in our way. Each week, when the running time was up, each of us would just sort of peel off and make for home. I usually headed home past the burger stand. Since it didn't open until eleven, there wasn't much chance of meeting any of the kids from school there.

This Saturday, though, I noticed a knot of kids hanging around in front as I approached. It was already too late to swerve off in another direction, so I just hoped there wouldn't be anyone I knew. I was wearing my baggy blue-and-white jogging suit and I was red-faced and sweaty, my hair sticking out in corkscrews in all directions and some of it hanging down in my eyes like a sheepdog's.

Sure enough, one of them recognized me.

"Oh, my goodness!" she shrieked as I got nearer. "Look, look, it's Glenda."

At first I was almost relieved to see that it was Mary Lou. Then I saw that she was with Cathanne and two boys I didn't know. And standing a little bit away from the group, half-sitting on his bike near the curb, was Roddy Fenton.

I came to a halt in front of Mary Lou, gulping for breath.

"Oh," Mary Lou said, looking very distressed. "You must be so *hot*. I just don't see how you *stand* it."

Cathanne tossed her head so her hair shimmered in the sun. "Honestly, Mary Lou, some people don't

59

mind exerting themselves a little." Her eyes gave me a quick once-over. "You're looking good, Glenda. Getting in condition, huh?"

"Yes," I said cautiously. The two boys had drifted away from Cathanne and Mary Lou and were now talking in low voices to Roddy over near the curb. Were they talking about me? I couldn't tell. "I'm just on my way home," I panted. "Been out for a couple of hours."

Cathanne kept looking at me. "I've been thinking of starting to do some running myself."

Mary Lou looked alarmed. "Don't you usually go jogging with Patty, Glenda?" You could see she was trying to keep Cathanne away from me.

I shook my head. "Uh-uh. Patty doesn't run at all. I go alone most days."

"Maybe I'll go with you sometime," said Cathanne. "Give it a try."

"Sure," I said, wondering if she really meant it. My eye kept wandering uneasily toward Roddy and the other two boys.

"What are you two doing here, anyway?" I asked.

Cathanne did a little jig and winked at me. "Oh, just hanging out."

"And waiting for the burger place to open," Mary Lou added soberly. She looked at Cathanne. "Didn't you say we should come down here and get something cool to drink?"

"That's right," Cathanne said with a teasing smile.

"So who are those two boys talking to Roddy?" I asked.

Cathanne shrugged. "Don't know. We only just got

here and were starting to talk to them when you came along."

"She's always looking for boys," Mary Lou said. She turned to Cathanne. "You know, I think that's the real reason you made me walk all the way down here."

Cathanne grinned. "Well, aren't you clever."

I watched the two boys suddenly walk away from Roddy and bang on the window of the burger stand. "Hey, open up. It's nearly eleven."

Some cars had begun driving into the parking lot.

"I better get home," I said. "Got to take a shower."

"I should think *so*," Mary Lou commented.

"Why don't you stay around and get a Coke?" Cathanne suggested. "You must be dying of thirst."

"I don't drink anything till after I'm done running," I said.

"Besides," Mary Lou added, "she only drinks diet stuff. Can't you tell she's trying to lose weight?"

I glared at Mary Lou. She certainly had become nasty since her breakup with Patty and me.

"It so happens," I said, "I don't drink 'diet stuff' either. I only drink water. Anyhow, I don't have any money with me, so good-by."

"What's your rush?" Roddy had strolled over. "I'll buy you a drink if you're thirsty."

"I'm *not* thirsty," I half yelled at Roddy.

All through my conversation with Cathanne and Mary Lou I'd had the feeling they were looking at me as though I were some kind of freak. Fat Glenda, the town joke, trying to get thin. All I needed now was for Roddy to start taunting me.

I didn't say another word. I began to make tracks

for home. As soon as I was away from the burger stand, I started running at a faster pace than usual.

"Hey, wait up," said a voice at my side. "I can't even bike that fast."

It was Roddy again. I just kept on running.

"What's wrong? You sore at me, Glenda?"

I shook my head no. I just wished he'd go away.

"You know," Roddy said, biking alongside me now, close to the curb, "I've really got to hand it to you, Glenda. When you make up your mind about something, you really go to it."

I was too winded to answer him. And I didn't know if he was being sincere or not, just the way I hadn't been able to tell with Cathanne.

But Roddy kept right on talking. "So how many pounds do you expect to lose? I mean have you got a regular program or what?"

I came to a street crossing and dashed over to the other side even though a car was coming pretty fast. Ordinarily I wouldn't have. I'd have waited and jogged in place.

But of course I didn't lose Roddy. He caught up with me again and went right on talking. "Boy, you're fast, you know that? I wouldn't think somebody like you . . . well, you know, a girl and all . . ."

That did it. I swung my arm around the trunk of a small tree to stop myself. "Okay," I puffed at him. "The last time I spoke to you in the schoolyard, I thought maybe you'd grown up a little. But I see you're the same pesty kid you always were."

Roddy's hand went up in self-defense, as though he expected me to hit him. "Whoa," he grinned, his voice suddenly going into a very deep register. "What'd I do? What'd I say?"

"Listen," I panted, "don't give me that 'innocent' stuff. Harmless little you. You always *were* out to get me. You even tried to get my best friend Sara away from me. You think I forgot all that stuff just 'cause it happened a year ago?"

Roddy gave me a baffled laugh. "Hey, Glenda, what's wrong with you? Your brains musta gotten all shook up from so much running."

"There's nothing wrong with my brains," I told him. "I haven't forgotten *anything* that ever happened between us. And I especially haven't forgotten what happened the first week of school *this* year!"

"The first week of school?" Roddy scratched his head. "What are you talking about? I'm not even in any of your classes."

"It didn't happen *in* school," I shot back. "It happened in the street. In a street very much like this one."

Roddy clapped both hands to his head. "What did? What?" This time his voice broke into a falsetto squeal.

"You called me a name. You saw me out running, dressed like I am now." I grabbed the sleeve of my jogging suit. "And you went speeding past me on your bike and you yelled out, 'Hey Jelly Belly!' "

"Jelly Belly?" Roddy acted like he had just been knocked out and immediately collapsed onto the handlebars of his bike. He went into a fit of raucous laughter. "Jelly Belly?" He laughed so hard tears came to his eyes. "Hey, Glenda, what a thing to say. I never. Listen"—he raised his right hand—"I never." Suddenly

63

his hand shot out and he pointed a finger at me. "Prove it. I dare you. Just prove it."

"I haven't got any witnesses," I stormed at him. "But I don't need any. I *know* you said it. I just know you're the one."

Roddy stared at me open-mouthed for a moment. "You know what? You're crazy. You think you haven't got any friends because you're fat. But I'll tell you why you haven't. It's because you're crazy."

"Listen," I shrilled at him, "I don't need friends. And I certainly don't need friends like you. So just leave me alone, will you!"

I was close to exploding into angry tears.

Without another word, Roddy wheeled around on his bike, pedaled furiously down the street, and disappeared around the corner.

9

"Glenda," Mr. Hartley said, softly tapping the edge of my desk with a pencil. "Can you stay a minute after class today? I'll give you a note to your next class if you're late."

"It'll be okay," I whispered. "I only have study hall after English on Wednesdays."

"Good." He smiled and went on with the lesson.

It wasn't the first time Mr. Hartley had asked me to stay so he could give me a batch of exam papers to mark. I was really flattered and, of course, I loved doing things for him. His taking special notice of me had all begun, I realized, after I'd reported on my love poem:

> *If thou must love me, let it be for naught*
> *Except for love's sake only . . .*

Today Mr. Hartley gave me thirty ninth-grade short-answer tests on Shakespeare to mark. Ninth-grade papers, while I was only in eighth. That made me feel pretty good.

When I got to study hall, I took a seat way over by myself and began to check the papers against the answer sheet. Mr. Hartley had told me I should initial each finished paper with a D.H. It really gave me a thrill to write those two letters even though I *still* didn't know what the *D* stood for.

I wondered if I'd ever be able to think of him as Dustin or Derek or Darren or whatever his first name was. I was so used to *Mr.* Hartley. It was a beautiful second name, and romantic too. "Hart" *was,* after all, very close to "heart."

I was just finishing the fourth or fifth paper, lovingly inscribing a D.H. at the bottom, when Patty came shuffling along the row of seats toward me. She sank down into the seat beside me.

"Teacher's pet, huh?" she whispered.

I stared at her indignantly.

Her eyes crinkled into a smile. "Oh, come on, Glenda. I was only joking." She put her hand on my arm. "Gee, you're so touchy lately. I guess dieting makes people very edgy."

"I'm not edgy," I said, trying to act perfectly cool. "I didn't ask Mr. Hartley to give me papers to mark. He just started doing it. It's not hard, so why should I refuse?"

"I know," Patty said soothingly. "I didn't mean anything bad by it. Or about dieting, either. You *are* getting

66

thinner, you know. I saw you from a short distance away the other day and I wasn't sure it was you."

I looked at her. Why was she trying to be so nice?

"You're losing weight real fast now, aren't you, Glenda?" she said, with what seemed like genuine admiration. "I honestly think you're terrific, eating plain unflavored yogurt or a hard-boiled egg for lunch every day with all those raw vegetables. How much have you lost already?"

"I don't know," I replied. "I found out it isn't a good idea to weigh yourself too often. If you're not losing, you get discouraged, and if you are losing, you begin to get careless."

Patty nodded slowly. "I see. I never thought about it that way."

She sank down lower in her seat. "Glenda," she breathed in a very soft voice, "do you know what today is?"

What a strange question. "Wednesday," I said absently, starting to check the next paper.

"I mean the date, the date."

"It's the last week in October," I remarked, "the twenty-something. Why?"

"Why?" Patty exclaimed, suddenly clutching my arm. "Because it's almost, nearly, practically . . . Halloween."

"Halloween? Oh, don't talk to me about that."

"Why not?"

"Don't you remember last year? There were big kids roaming around town in cars throwing eggs. They threw eggs all over Sara's house. This town gets crazy

67

on Halloween. I had such a great costume for trick-or-treating, and then at the last minute Sara and I had a fight, which was all Roddy Fenton's fault, and I didn't even get to wear it."

"What was it?" Patty wanted to know.

"Snow White," I said. "It was made out of my mother's old white bedsheets because I was so awfully, awfully fat at that time. But I had a rhinestone belt and high-heeled silver shoes with rhinestone buckles and a long blonde wig. And I was going to wear glitter dust on my eyelids."

"It sounds wonderful," Patty said. "Why don't you wear it this year?"

"To what?" I asked numbly.

"To go trick-or-treating," Patty suggested.

"You must be crazy. That's kiddie stuff. Besides what would I want with collecting a lot of candy?"

Patty sucked at the tip of her pinkie. "I guess you're right," she said. "You know what would be really nice? If somebody made a party. A Halloween party."

"And invited us, of course."

"Of course."

"Well, I don't really care about Halloween this year," I told Patty. "I expect to be a lot thinner by Thanksgiving. I just hope the auditions for Mr. Hartley's show are as late in November as possible."

I'd broken my vow and mentioned the auditions to Patty. But I didn't care. After all, if she was supposed to be my friend, I was supposed to be able to talk to her about the things that were on my mind, wasn't I?

This time Patty acted surprisingly warm. "I watched

you in dancercise class yesterday, Glenda. You were *so* good. I'll bet you do get into the show."

She sounded sincere, but I still had the feeling she was trying to butter me up.

"If I did get in," I said, "and that's still a very big *if*, it wouldn't have anything to do with my marking papers for Mr. Hartley, you understand. One thing doesn't have anything to do with the other."

"Of course not," Patty said solemnly. But she seemed to be thinking of something else. After a little while she said, "Well, what *about* Halloween, Glenda?"

"What do you mean what about it? I told you I don't care."

"What if you did care, though? If you wanted awfully to go to a party and nobody invited you, would you maybe think of making one yourself?"

"I see," I said slowly. "So you're thinking of making a Halloween party."

"I *thought* of it," Patty said. "But I can't. See, I'd have wanted to make it on Saturday night so we could stay up late, but my parents are going out, and they won't let me have a party unless they're around to supervise."

"What about Friday night?" I asked. "That's just as good."

"Same thing," Patty said almost mournfully. "You have such a nice house, Glenda. I don't suppose . . ."

I realized at once what Patty was driving at. Was that why she had been complimenting me on my dancing and praising the way I was losing weight?

"My house," I exclaimed. "Forget it. I never told

69

you, but I really caught it from my mother that day you and Mary Lou came over and walked on the living room carpet with wet feet. She had to have the rug shampooed. I think she's still angry about it."

"Oh," Patty said, her eyes widening. "I didn't know. I'm sorry. You should have said something. Anyhow, I didn't mean for you to have the party in the living room. I was thinking about the den. Or maybe you have a finished basement?"

I shook my head no. When I was little, my mother had always made parties for me and invited all the kids in the neighborhood so I'd be popular. But it had never worked. So I'd decided a few years ago that fat Glenda wasn't going to give any more parties, at least not while she was still fat.

Patty slouched even deeper into her seat. "Too bad," she murmured. "I just know Cathanne's going to get invited to something, and Mary Lou will tag along 'cause she's attached herself to Cathanne. And you and I," she sighed, raising her eyes to the flaking, beige-painted, study-hall ceiling, "will be left high and dry."

A couple of days later I came on a strange sight on my way to the English class. Patty was standing in the school corridor having what looked like a serious discussion with fat Robert. They looked so odd together because he towered above her and she had to bend her head far, far back to look up at him. Even odder than that, I'd also noticed them talking to each other in the classroom the day before.

I just nodded and walked past them into the room.

But as Patty came by my desk a few minutes later, I couldn't keep myself from tugging at her sleeve and whispering, "What was all that about?"

She smiled mysteriously and said, "You'll see."

I tugged harder.

"You'll *see*," she repeated. "And when you do, you'll realize what a really good friend I am. You'll say I'm the best you ever had."

Meantime fat Robert had also entered the room and had gone over to talk quietly to Mr. Hartley. What was going on?

It was hard to concentrate during the lesson. Once or twice I actually found myself in a kind of trance. I was eating very little these days. Maybe I was faint with hunger and didn't even know it. I did know that I was getting thinner. I was wearing a belt with my jeans now, and every few days I had to change the notch to make it tighter. At home in my room I'd even experimented with tucking my blouse inside my pants instead of wearing it outside. And it worked! Of course, I still had a long way to go. But at least I was on my way.

A few minutes before the period was about to end, Mr. Hartley beckoned to Robert. "Okay," he said, "let's do it now."

I spun to attention. Was this what Patty had been talking about?

Robert came walking heavily to the front of the room. He took a piece of colored chalk and began to write something on the blackboard using the side of the chalk so the lines came out broad and cottony. I began

71

to realize he was writing an address—a house number—and the name of a street.

Then he turned to the class and cleared his throat like the time he'd gotten up to read his poem.

"I have," Robert said in a very loud, formal voice, "an announcement to make. We're going to have an English-class Halloween party a week from Saturday night. At *my* house." Robert pointed to the address on the blackboard behind him. "Everybody in the class is invited. But . . . there's one rule. It's a costume party. You can't come without a costume and a mask."

Following the surprise of most of the kids in the class, there was a lot of cheering and some hooting.

Robert held up his hands for quiet.

"And," he turned to look at Mr. Hartley, "you didn't hear the best part. Even though he can't spend the whole evening with us, Mr. Hartley has graciously consented to put in an appearance and judge the most original costume!"

I turned around to look at Patty. She smiled and nodded to me, her eyes wide. So that was what she'd been up to. She'd talked Robert into making the Halloween party she wanted so much to go to.

I felt a momentary twinge of resentment toward Patty. I still remembered the way she'd made fun of Robert that day at my house. Had Patty figured she'd ask Robert because she thought most fat people were good-natured, or because he didn't have many friends and wanted to be popular?

Looking at Robert's broadly smiling, satisfied face I began to wonder if he was as sensitive about these things as I was. Maybe, being a boy, he didn't have to be. Maybe we were just different people, even if we were both fat.

I glanced at Patty once again, shrugged, and forced a grin.

Now all I had to do was to figure out the most original idea for a Halloween costume. It certainly wasn't going to be Snow White!

10

That night I wrote a desperate letter to Sara.

> You're the smartest person of my age that I
> know. So please think hard and send me an idea
> for an original costume, something that nobody
> else in the whole crowd at the Halloween party
> will think of. If you get a good idea call me col-
> lect and I'll pay for it. There's not much time.
> Did I tell you that Mr. Hartley is coming to the
> party? It has to be a beautiful costume, not some-
> thing funny or goofy. I want to look . . . gor-
> geous!

Just as I was finishing the letter, I heard the phone
ring.

"It's for you, Glenda," my mother said, poking her
head in the door of my room. She was clutching a
handful of celery sticks to appease what she called her

"mid-evening hunger," which sometimes struck between dinner and bedtime snack. "That friend with the Southern accent."

Mary Lou! It had been ages since she'd phoned me, and I wasn't feeling too friendly toward her, especially since the day I'd met her and Cathanne at the burger place on my way home from jogging.

"Glenda," she said, sounding very apologetic, "I hope I haven't interrupted your homework. I just had to talk to you."

"It's okay," I said grumpily. "What's up."

"What's *up?* Well, just everybody's talking about it. How can you ask?"

"Just the same," I said impatiently, "I'm asking. What's everybody talking about?"

"Well, the party, of course. The Halloween party. The one Mr. Hartley's coming to."

"Oh," I said with some surprise, "are you coming to that?"

"Well, of course I am. If I can think of a costume. Why wouldn't I?"

"I don't know," I said slowly. "Patty . . . um, seemed to think you and Cathanne had already been invited to some other party."

"Where'd she get that idea? She hardly ever even talks to Cathanne and me. Anyhow, even if I did get invited to another party, I wouldn't go to it. I'd go to this one. There's only one problem."

"What's that?"

"What will I wear? What costume? Glenda, you're really clever. You picked the best love poem, remember? You've *got* to help me."

"Oh, for heaven's sake, Mary Lou, how can I help

you? I don't even know what *I'm* going to wear. You think it's easy to dream up an original, prize-winning costume?"

"But listen, mine doesn't have to be prize-winning, just good *enough*. Know what I mean?"

"Why don't you ask Cathanne?"

"O-h-h-h," Mary Lou drawled, "I'm fed up with Cathanne. Know what she does, Glenda? She *uses* me, that's what. She makes me go places with her, like that day at the burger stand. She walks me all over town hunting for boys. She's so boy crazy. And then when she finds some, she forgets all about me. She just leaves me on the sidelines feeling real dumb."

"Well, is she coming to the party at Robert's house?"

"I don't even know. See, we had a kind of spat just the other day. Because I told her how I felt. And she said if I didn't like it, I could just quit hanging around her like a leech. A leech! Isn't that disgustin'?"

I could see now why Mary Lou was phoning me. I should have been angrier at her, but she really was a sad soul.

"Well, listen," I said, "what costumes have you got? What did you wear last year when you went trick-or-treating?"

"Oh, that," Mary Lou replied. "It's so ordinary. It's a tall, pointy black hat with a big floppy brim. I wore it with a long black cloak. Everybody'll think I'm a witch. Or maybe Mother Goose."

I thought a while. "Have you still got the cloak, Mary Lou?"

"Um hmmm."

"Have you got a long flannel nightgown with a high neck?"

"Um hmmm."

"Have you got a pair of bedroom slippers?"

"Um hmmm."

"Got a candle?"

"I guess so. My goodness, Glenda, what sort of costume is that?"

"Listen carefully now," I said. "Forget the hat and wear your hair loose and flowing and sort of mussed up like you were sleeping and you got out of bed in the middle of the night. Wear the bedroom slippers and the nightgown and throw the cloak over your shoulders. Carry the candle in some kind of candleholder and put splotches of blood all over your hands."

Mary Lou screeched. "Eeek! Blood."

"Not *real* blood. You paint red blobs all over your hands with blood-red nail polish."

"But why?" Mary Lou demanded. "Who am I?"

"You're Lady Macbeth, you dope. It's the sleep-walking scene. She's a murderess wandering around the castle in the middle of the night, trying to get the blood off her hands and saying, 'Out damned spot! Out, I say!' "

"Lady Macbeth!" Mary Lou gasped. "But we don't even study Shakespeare until ninth grade."

I rolled my eyes to the ceiling. "What's that got to do with it? Mr. Hartley will know and so will everybody else. It's one of Shakespeare's most famous plays."

I suppose all those Shakespeare short-answer tests I'd been marking for Mr. Hartley lately had really taken hold in my mind because the Lady Macbeth idea had come to me almost automatically.

"You're right," Mary Lou said, actually starting to

sound enthusiastic. "Glenda, I think it's a wonderful idea. But . . ."

"But what?"

"But do you think my mother will let me wear my nightgown? To a party?"

"Why not? Put on your regular underwear. You could even wear jeans underneath if she's worried."

"And . . . and how will I get the blood off my hands?"

"Listen, Mary Lou," I said with exasperation, "I just gave you the best idea in the whole world for an original costume that Mr. Hartley is going to *love*. I don't even know why I did it. I could have kept the idea for myself. You want to know how you get the blood off your hands? You get it off with nail-polish remover. The next day. *After* you win first prize. Any more foolish questions?"

"No. Oh, Glenda, I *love* you! You're the best friend a person could ask for. I'll never forget you for this. Never!"

Mary Lou hung up the phone in a flurry of little smacking noises that I supposed were kisses. I'd never heard her so excited.

I sat there thinking. What had I done? I'd just had a brainstorm, gotten the best idea I was ever going to get for a prize-winning original costume, and I'd given it away to Mary Lou!

The moment I saw Patty's face at Miss Esme's Tuesday afternoon dancercise class, I knew something was wrong.

I was feeling depressed enough as it was. The whole weekend had gone by, the party was only a few more days away, and I still hadn't been able to think of a really great costume for myself. No phone call from Sara yet, either.

Still, I wasn't too sorry I'd given the Lady Macbeth idea to Mary Lou. Because now that I was thinner I'd decided I didn't want to wear some loose, baggy outfit made out of sheets or a nightgown. I wanted something really sleek and glamorous. I wanted people—and especially Mr. Hartley—to see a really different me at the party.

That afternoon Miss Esme started the class with a warm-up number that we all knew pretty well by now. But twice Patty bumped into me, and the third time she landed a sharp kick on my ankle.

"Hey!" I panted. "Watch it."

"You're the one who's out of step," she breathed.

"Am not. Anyhow, there's lots of space, so move off."

"Move yourself."

We seemed to be having a fight.

When the number ended, Miss Esme began teaching us a new routine. Patty and I didn't have a chance to say another word to each other. We didn't even look at one another until the break.

"Well, you're in a fine mood today," she said sarcastically.

"Me? You're the one who kicked me in the ankle."

Patty pushed her hair back from her forehead and plopped herself down on the floor crosslegged.

"I ought to kick you right in the head, Glenda." Her eyes were blazing.

"What's wrong with you? Are you crazy?" I looked

around. A few of the people in the class were staring at Patty.

"Yes, crazy to ever have been a friend of yours. What kind of a lousy double-crosser are you?"

"I don't know what you're talking about. And I think you'd better watch your language."

"I'll say what I please. You deserve a lot worse." She glared at me. *"Lady Macbeth!"*

"Oh," I said, almost with relief, "so Mary Lou's been going around blabbing about her costume."

"Not exactly," Patty said. "I had to drag it out of her. At first all she said was that you'd given her the greatest idea in the world." Patty suddenly looked close to tears. "How could you do it, Glenda? I'm the one who got Robert to agree to make the party and to ask Mr. Hartley to be there. I'm the one who engineered the whole deal. Mary Lou isn't your best friend. What's *wrong* with you?"

"I didn't do it on purpose," I protested. "It . . . well, it just happened. She phoned me and she told me about the trouble she was having with Cathanne and she . . . she just seemed a natural for the part. You'd have been too short for Lady Macbeth. For heaven's sake, Patty, I don't even have a costume for myself."

"Oh," Patty said, without much sympathy, "you'll think of something. But what about me? You really owe me a suggestion, Glenda. And I don't mean Snow White, either."

I scratched my head. I was in a fine pickle, having to think up great costumes for everybody else. But to be perfectly fair, maybe Patty did have a point. I *was* closer friends with her than I was with Mary Lou.

"Um, let's see," I said solemnly.

Patty clambered onto her knees, then sat back on her heels, her hands clasped in front of her, her eyes glittering.

"Well?" she prompted. "Well?"

"Just a sec. Even geniuses have to think a minute."

"Come on, come on," she urged. "Break time's almost over."

I snapped my fingers. "I think it should be another character out of Shakespeare, don't you? Mr. Hartley would be really tuned in to that."

"Okay," Patty said breathlessly. "But who? Not one of the witches from *Macbeth*. Everybody always expects witches on Halloween."

"No," I said, thinking hard. "Not *Macbeth*. A different play. O-O-O-Ophelia!"

Patty looked disappointed. "I never heard of that one."

"That's the character, dopey. It's from *Hamlet*. She's the one who goes mad and is drowned."

"So what do I wear? A bathing suit?"

"Very funny," I said. "You wear the clothes from the mad scene. A long white dress, gauzy. Or I could lend you my old Snow White sheets and my rhinestone belt. A wreath on your head, sitting sort of lopsided, and flowers in your hands—rosemary for remembrance, pansies, violets, columbines, and rue, whatever that is. We could look up the part in the play where she says all those things."

Patty seemed doubtful. "I don't know. Lady Macbeth sounds better."

Just then Miss Esme called out to us. "Do you girls want to talk or dance?"

I jumped to my feet. "I told you before," I whispered, "you're too short for Lady Macbeth. Anyhow, you're sure to make a hit because Ophelia is one of Mr. Hartley's favorite characters."

"How do you know?"

"I know," I assured her. "She's on all his short-answer tests."

11

"I'm going to ask Miss Esme," Patty said, "and see what she thinks."

The dancercise class had just ended.

"About Ophelia?"

"Not exactly. Come with me," Patty urged.

Miss Esme was over at the stereo machine sorting the records she'd played during the class.

"Hi," she said in a friendly way as we approached. "I've been meaning to tell you girls you're both looking very good on the floor. Glenda, you're moving better every session. That thin 'you' inside is really beginning to assert herself."

I blushed a little and smiled thinking of Sara's poem, the one she'd sent me last summer:

> *Remember, Glenda,*
> *I have no doubt*

83

*There's a thin you inside
That will get out!*

All I said was, "Thanks." Patty said nothing.

Miss Esme drew her brows together. "Anything I can do for you girls? Some problem?"

Patty gave me a wide-eyed look.

"Well, go ahead," I told her. "You said you were going to ask."

Miss Esme was distracted for a moment as some of the other people in the class left and waved good-by.

She turned back to us. "Ask me what?"

Patty looked down at her feet. "Oh, it's a dumb question, I guess. We . . . I . . . just wanted to know if you had any good ideas for a costume to wear to a Halloween party. See, our whole English class is going to be there and . . . and the thing is our English teacher, Mr. Hartley, is going to judge the most original costume."

Miss Esme looked serious. "That's a big order. Haven't you been able to think of anything?"

I looked at Patty. "I gave her a good idea but she isn't sure she likes it. I'm the one who really has the problem. But . . . well, I'll think of something. I guess."

"I'm sure you will," Miss Esme said with a faint smile. "Anything else?"

"Well, yes," Patty said, as though she'd just remembered. "Our English teacher, this Mr. Hartley, is also going to direct the school show this year. Auditions are next month. And Glenda and I, we just wondered, if you could help us work up some kind of dance number, something catchy and not too hard that we could do for the tryouts."

Miss Esme lit up a little. "What kind of show is it?"

"Oh," I explained quickly, "it's a musical revue. Songs, dances, skits, magic acts." I turned to Patty. "Isn't that right?"

She shrugged. "I guess. Mr. Hartley said we should come to the tryouts and show him what we can do. He says if we have some talent he'll put our number in the show."

Miss Esme drew her eyebrows together again. This time a needlelike line appeared between her eyes. "Did you say his name is Hartley? What does he look like?"

I glanced at Patty and we both grinned.

"Oh, super," she said with a mischievous smile.

"Tall, with broad shoulders and golden-brown hair and the bluest eyes you ever saw," I gushed. "I guess he's about, um, thirty, thirty-two. He looks like . . . an actor."

"Really?" Miss Esme looked very interested. I'd never seen her face so alive before. "Does he have an acting background?"

We both shrugged. Then I remembered something. "He said he was a director, but a lazy one. He said he wasn't going to be doing much coaching for the show."

Miss Esme made a face, but it was hard to figure out what her expression meant. "That sounds just like him," she said in a flat tone, as though she were talking to herself. Then she looked directly at me. "Your English teacher's name wouldn't be David Hartley, would it?"

"David. Oh!"

Miss Esme and Patty both gave me a puzzled look.

"The *D*," I explained. "I never knew what his initial stood for. I thought maybe Dustin or Derek. But David's a nice name, too."

"It means 'beloved,'" Miss Esme said matter-of-factly.

"Beloved," I murmured, thinking how well that went with the "heart" from Hartley.

Luckily my romantic simpering was drowned out by Patty's squealing. "You *know* him? Ooh, maybe you could put in a good word for us at auditions." She caught herself. "I'm just kidding."

Miss Esme sighed. "Well, if he's the same David Hartley I worked with on an off-Broadway musical a couple of years ago, then I know him. I do recall word going around that he had once studied to be an English teacher. It's a small world, though, his turning up here at Havenhurst Junior High."

Patty gave me a happy smile. "Wow, this is lucky for us. Did you dance in his show?" she asked Miss Esme.

"No, no. I choreographed it. I devised and arranged the dance numbers. It was David's first directorial job. He'd done some dancing in Broadway shows, chorus work, before that. But . . . well, that's a tough life and a short one. So he decided he'd try to get into directing."

Patty and I squeezed each other's arms. This was so exciting, getting all the inside information on Mr. Hartley. Even Cathanne couldn't possibly know this much.

"I'll bet he was a terrific dancer," Patty said. "And was he a good director, too?"

"I never actually saw him dance in a show," Miss Esme replied. "And that off-Broadway collaboration was the only time I worked with him. It was . . . an experience."

"Good or bad?"

"A little of both," Miss Esme answered cryptically. "Let's just say the show folded a few weekends later. Then I heard he was directing something off-off-Broadway. That means a little more experimental," she explained.

"Why do you think he went back to teaching English?" I asked Miss Esme.

She shrugged. "Maybe he finally got the theater out of his system. Or maybe he's just filling in time until some new opportunity comes along. All I can say," she added wistfully, "is Havenhurst's a long way from Broadway."

Miss Esme unplugged the stereo and switched off a couple of the studio lights. "Well, I guess you girls want to get home. It's been nice chatting with you."

It wasn't until we were walking home in the chill autumn twilight that Patty remembered that Miss Esme had never said if she would help us work up a dance number for the audition.

"Let's be sure to ask her next time," Patty suggested.

"Um," I agreed. But my mind was on other things. "I wonder what she meant about Havenhurst being a long way from Broadway."

"Just what she said," Patty answered. "It is far. Sixty or seventy miles, I think."

I shook my head. "She meant it some other way. And I think she was also talking about herself somehow. All those years after she closed her old studio in town she must have been working in the theater, too.

But she finally decided to give it up and come back here. Why?"

Patty didn't seem to be listening to me at all.

"It's too bad really," she remarked, staring down at the sidewalk, "that she didn't have any ideas for a Halloween costume. I guess I didn't really expect her to."

"Oh, what are *you* worrying about?" I grumbled. "I already told you. Ophelia. I'm the one who's in big trouble. Four days to the party and my costume is still a complete mystery to me."

"Glenda!" my mother said, with a strange throb in her voice.

"What?" I turned around startled. It was the next day, and I had just come home from school and dumped my books on the kitchen table. My mother had her car keys in her hand and seemed to be on her way somewhere.

"I couldn't believe my eyes just now," she said. "It was the strangest sensation."

"What was?"

My mother sank into a kitchen chair. "Well, I got a glimpse of you as you turned around to put your books down and suddenly . . . well, it just wasn't my Glenda anymore. Do you know," she said, leaning forward with an intense expression on her face, "that you're getting *very* thin?"

Suddenly I saw that there were tears in her eyes. And the moment I saw them, there were tears in mine, too. She opened her arms and I ran into them.

"Oh, my baby," she wept, "what's become of you? What's become of my Glenda?"

After a while I pulled away from her and smiled, even though I was still misty-eyed. It really seemed to be happening at last, exactly what Sara had predicted in her poem:

> *Just start shedding pounds*
> *And folks'll soon wonder,*
> *Whatever became of . . .*
> > *Fat Glenda?*

"I'm still here," I said reassuringly. "There's still plenty of me."

"You're starting to have a lovely figure, too," my mother said admiringly. "Oh, I'm so proud of my little girl. And you're doing it all yourself. I know Miss Esme's classes are helping. But when it comes to food, your will power is just phenomenal. I only hope you're getting enough to grow on. You eat so *little*."

"I'm okay," I said. "You don't need to worry about me."

My mother unclicked her handbag and dabbed at her eyes with a filmy handkerchief. "I do worry though," she said. "You know that."

A few moments later she stood up, still sniffling a little.

"Listen, dear, I've got to cart a whole bunch of stuff over to the county hall for the bazaar and rummage sale this weekend. So much to do. But I'll be back before dinnertime. I'm hungry this minute from that skimpy lunch I had, but I won't eat a thing now. I've really got to try to follow your example."

If anything, my mother had put on a little weight in the last few months. I watched her sidle out the door and into her car. For the first time I found myself feeling truly sorry for her and her losing battle. How *could* she lose weight? What really good reason did she have? There was no David Hartley in her life. David, which meant . . . "beloved."

I was still musing, as I had been since yesterday afternoon, on what Miss Esme had told Patty and me about Mr. Hartley. I guess I'd actually fallen into a daydream because, when the back doorbell rang urgently, I was really jolted.

I glanced through the kitchen window and saw a strange car parked in our driveway. A woman's face appeared close to the glass pane in the back door.

"Sally Langridge, dear," she called out. I recognized her. She was a friend of my mother's and she seemed to be in a terrific hurry. In fact, she was tapping impatiently on the glass with a long enameled fingernail as I opened the door.

Mrs. Langridge was a striking brunette with high cheekbones and lots of eye makeup. "I missed her, didn't I?" she said breathlessly. "I told Grace I'd try to get over here by three with all that stuff for the rummage sale. But," she glanced at her watch, "as usual, I'm running behind time."

I looked past her toward the car.

"Yes, the rummage," she said. "Is it all right if I unload it and leave it here? It's an awful lot, I'm afraid. But this time I promised myself I'd get rid of it."

"Should I help you?" I offered.

"Oh, yes. If you would."

I went out to the car with Mrs. Langridge. She opened the trunk. It was crammed with cartons and shopping bags heaped to overflowing with old clothes and bric-a-brac. Immediately, something lying on top of one of the shopping bags caught my eye. It was a long, hot-pink scarf made entirely of feathers, coiled round and round like a giant snake.

Nobody I knew wore scarves made of feathers around their necks. I was so fascinated I couldn't resist touching it. I gingerly lifted one end. The rosy feathers danced languidly in the air. Mrs. Langridge laughed.

"Isn't that boa marvelous?" she said. She looked at me. "Yes, it's called a boa, as in 'boa constrictor.' I hate giving some of these things away. But my husband said either we clean out the basement or move. What choice did I have?"

Mrs. Langridge had picked up the boa, uncoiled it, and hung it around her neck, flinging up one end so that it wound around twice. Then she unwound it and dropped it to her shoulders. Then, dropping it even further, she looped the boa around her hips, drew it tight, and did a quick little shimmy and a bump. "Awful, aren't I?" she giggled.

"Where'd you get it?" I asked in bewilderment.

"Oh, I never really wore it," she said quickly. "Except on the stage. Didn't your mother mention it? These are all bits and pieces of costumes and props from when we used to have an amateur Little Theater group in Havenhurst. Ages ago. When the group folded, everything somehow got stowed in my basement."

Mrs. Langridge and I made four or five trips and finally got all the boxes and bags neatly lined up in the hallway between the kitchen and the den.

"Thanks so much for helping me, dear," Mrs. Langridge said, as she hurried out the door. "By the way, you're growing up awfully pretty. And slimming down considerably. Did you know that?"

I grinned shyly as she got into her car with a wave that was more like a flourish.

"Ah," she called out cheerfully, as though she were making one of her stage exits, "ah, to be young again!"

12

Long after Mrs. Langridge had left, her perfume lingered in the air. The boa again lay on top of one of the shopping bags in the hall, and every time I walked past it a few feathers floated up gracefully and seemed to wave at me like tiny arms.

I picked up the coiling mass of fluff, went into my parents' room, and sat down at my mother's dressing table. I wrapped the boa around my neck twice, as Mrs. Langridge had done, and looked at myself in the mirror. The hot-pink feathers and my crinkly red-blond hair made a wild combination, drowning out my face so that it looked like a pale blob. What I needed, I decided, was a little makeup.

My mother's dressing table drawers were full of cosmetics, most of which she never used. She was always going to makeup demonstrations at various clubs and organizations, buying wrinkle creams and eyeshadow and lip liners and blushers—especially blushers—that were supposed to change the contours of your face. At least that was what the makeup demonstrators always told you they would do.

I studied my face in the mirror for a few minutes and decided to start right in. First, I sucked in my cheeks and rubbed the hollows with a brownish-pink paste to make them look as though they were in shadow. Then I highlighted the upper parts of my cheeks with a bright rosy-pink blusher that left a shiny gleam. I outlined my lips with a hot-pink liner that almost matched the boa and then filled in the rest of them with a glossy deep-pink lipstick that was just a shade lighter than the outline I'd drawn.

My eyes were next. I did them in four shades of blue—silver-blue near the lash line, deep-sea blue on the main part of the lid, storm-cloud blue in the crease of the lid, and pale-sky blue between the lid and the eyebrow for highlighting.

I leaned back. The effect was really sensational. My eyes were bigger, my cheeks were thinner, my freckles were hidden, and my lips looked positively luscious!

There was one thing left to do—my eyebrows. I found a velvet-brown eyebrow pencil and drew wide arching brows over my paler golden ones. Then, without really thinking about it, I stuck the tip of the eyebrow pencil against my cheek just under the tail of my right eye and twirled it around to make a dark-brown beauty spot.

The effect was perfect. The beauty spot looked absolutely right with the fluffy feather boa wound around my neck. I don't know where I'd gotten the idea. Maybe I'd seen somebody looking like that in an old movie on TV. I couldn't remember exactly.

I got up from the dressing table and began to walk around feeling really fantastic. Then I caught a glimpse of myself in my mother's full-length mirror and, of course, from the neck down everything was wrong. You can't wear a checked shirt, sloppy blue jeans, and clumsy gum-soled shoes with a hot-pink feather boa and a great-looking makeup job.

So I got to wondering. If the boa was part of the Havenhurst Little Theater's onetime costumes, what else was in those bags and boxes that Mrs. Langridge had donated for the rummage sale? Without wasting another second, I made a mad dash for the shopping bags in the hall and began tearing through them in a frenzy.

By the time my mother walked in the door an hour later, here's what I was wearing: a tight red-satin low-necked blouse with big floppy ruffles around the sleeves, which ended at the elbow, a short frilly red petticoat under a flared black taffeta skirt that was tight at the hips and came just to my kneecaps, black net stockings, and red satin shoes with high curved heels.

"Glenda!" my mother gasped, as I came toward her in the kitchen. She clutched at her chest. "What's all this? Haven't I already had enough of a shock for one day?"

I grinned at her.

"Where'd you get that costume? All that makeup. You know what you look like? I'd hate to tell you what you look like."

I pouted. "You mean it doesn't look . . . good?"

"Good? Well . . . it's effective," she said, slowly taking off her coat. "It's . . . it's striking. It's different.

But," she extended her arms in a helpless gesture, "where can you go looking like that?"

"Can't you guess where?" I replied teasingly. "To the Halloween party at fat Robert's . . . I mean at Robert's house on Saturday night. I've got my costume at last. Isn't it great!"

I twirled in front of her watching my taffeta skirt flare out like a parasol, buoyed up by the thickly ruffled petticoat underneath.

My mother sat down at the kitchen table and put her hand to her head. "Where did all that stuff you're wearing come from if I may ask?"

"Mrs. Langridge was here," I said, pointing toward the shopping bags and cartons in the hallway. "She was sorry she missed you. It's okay, isn't it, if I use some of the rummage-sale things for my costume?"

My mother waved her hand. "Oh, I see. Sally Langridge's collection of old costumes from the Little Theater." She made a clicking sound with her tongue. "How much resale value can they have? I just hope some of the bric-a-brac she brought is decent."

My mother got up at once and started for the hallway to see what was in the cartons. But as she passed close to me, she stopped short and squinted hard at my beauty mark.

"I don't know, Glenda." She shook her head. "I just don't know. I can't imagine what your father will say when he walks in the door. To see you made up like a . . . a dance-hall queen . . ."

A dance-hall queen! All this time that I'd been parading around in my costume and makeup I hadn't really *known* what I was. Now at least I knew. My mother had put exactly the right name to it.

Patty was going to be Ophelia from *Hamlet,* Mary Lou was going to be Lady Macbeth, and I, Glenda, was going to be a dance-hall queen, the kind you saw in all those westerns on TV.

I threw my arms around my mother so hard I nearly knocked her off balance.

"Oh, I'm so happy! It's a terrific costume, isn't it? And I don't look fat in it, do I? Do you realize I might even win a prize? When Mr. Hartley sees me in this . . ."

My mother patted my bare shoulder gently. "Now, now, calm down a little, Glenda. You realize, of course, you'll have to have your father's permission to wear that costume. A dance-hall queen isn't exactly the nicest kind of woman for a young girl to impersonate—always hanging around the bar in those wild Old West saloons, mingling with shifty-eyed gamblers and dirty, rough-looking cattle rustlers. And those high-kicking dances they did when they entertained must have been pretty scandalous."

"Oh, Mom!" I burst out laughing. "All that stuff happened a hundred years ago. And there aren't going to be any cattle rustlers at the party, just the kids in my English class. And . . . and our English teacher," I added.

My mother smiled faintly. I could see she wasn't going to object strenuously to my dance-hall queen costume. And, as for my father, he'd never in his life stopped me from doing something unless my mother had told him to in the first place!

One thing I'd made up my mind about was that nobody in my class, but nobody, was going to know anything about my costume until the night of the party. So the next few days were really hard. Both Patty and Mary Lou pestered me for information, and even Cathanne sidled up to me as I was getting ready to leave the school lunchroom on Thursday, *after* she'd made sure that neither Patty nor Mary Lou was around.

"Glenda," she gushed, just as though we had always been close friends, "I have a real hard decision to make. I have two great costumes to wear to the party on Saturday night. And I just can't decide which one is better. I bet you could help me."

"What are they?" I asked innocently.

"Well, that would be telling, wouldn't it? I mean, if you have *two* great ideas you really have a double secret to keep, don't you?"

I stuck my hands on my hips. "But Cathanne," I said, "how can I give you an answer if I don't know the question?"

Cathanne curled her arm around my waist and lowered her voice to a confidential whisper. "Well, here's what I thought. If you already have your costume idea then you could tell me what it is and then I'd tell you my two. And maybe if we weren't crazy about our own ideas, we could swap." She looked around the lunchroom swiftly. "I think we carrot-tops really ought to stick together, don't you?" She gave my hair a friendly little tug.

I looked at her in real shock. "I'm sorry," I told her, "but that sounds crazy to me. Do you want to know what I think? I think we all ought to keep our costumes a secret until Saturday night. Oh, and don't forget to wear a mask, so no one will recognize you, and it'll be a real surprise."

98

Cathanne looked disappointed. Her eyes narrowed and she didn't say anything.

"I know," I added, "that some people around school have been blabbing that I gave them ideas for costumes. But I'm fresh out of ideas right now. And anyhow you said you had two."

"I have," she replied defiantly. "I could probably even have helped you, Glenda. If you'd wanted to be friendly, that is."

I sighed and gathered my books together. I knew Cathanne was dying to impress Mr. Hartley. I guess all of us were. I knew *I* was because, in a special way, I felt Mr. Hartley was "mine." It wasn't just because he'd liked my love poem the best or because he always asked me to mark papers for him. It was because, without his even knowing it, he'd helped me to lose pounds and pounds of fat. Just one electric-blue flash of his magical eyes and my appetite vanished for days.

When I got home from school that afternoon, I found a letter from Sara. It was too soon, of course, to expect her to have sent me a costume idea by mail, and luckily I didn't need one now. Sara had enclosed a new "pep" poem, for losing weight, though, which I could still use.

I thought it was one of the best poems she'd ever sent me. She wrote that she'd made it up after hearing that lots of people in California were buying tight bathing suits on purpose. Once they had the new bathing suit home, they'd start losing weight frantically so they could fit into it in time for the next big pool party.

I guess, with the weather being so nice in California, Sara had forgotten that where I lived there was a big difference between Halloween and the Fourth of July. In Havenhurst the weather was turning so cold that nobody was thinking of bathing suits at the moment.

But she meant well, and here's how the poem went:

> *If you hang your bikini*
> > *On the refrigerator door,*
> *The goodies inside*
> > *Will be easier to ignore!*

13

The first thing I saw when my father drove up to Robert's house was somebody hanging around out front dressed up as a wolf man. He was wearing a gray sweat suit with a tail attached and dirty gray sneakers. You could be absolutely sure this person was a wolf man because of the horrible mask he was wearing. It covered his entire head, hair and all, had fangs instead of teeth, and lots of blood dripping down onto its chin.

"This is the place for sure," I announced, reaching for the door handle of the car.

My father leaned across me and grabbed my hand.

"Just a minute, young lady. I'm not letting you out onto a pitch black street at a strange address with a hideous monster like that lurking around on the sidewalk."

"Oh," I said airily, "don't worry about him. I know

who that is. Although I'm not really sure what he's doing here since he isn't actually in our English class."

My father turned off the engine. "I'd better see you into the house. Your mother would never forgive me if I didn't."

I had to think fast.

"No," I begged. "If the kids at the party see you, or even if the wolf man does, they'll know right away who I am. So please, please stay in the car. And you can watch me go into the house. Okay?"

My father grunted, and this time I got out quickly. I had to be careful how I walked though. It wasn't just the high heels of those red satin shoes and the long black velvet cape my mother had lent me. It was also the mask I was wearing. It was black silk trimmed with sequins. And even though I'd cut out big, big openings so everyone could see my terrific four-shades-of-blue eye makeup, I couldn't see out of the corners too well.

I got up onto the sidewalk okay, and right away the wolf man came toward me.

"Hey, is that you, Cathanne? Gee, you look terrific. What an outfit."

I just nodded and put my finger on my lips.

The wolf man took my arm. "You're sure it's okay about my going in there. I still feel kind of funny about crashing the party."

I nodded again and headed up the path to the front door. There hadn't been any question in my mind right from the start that the wolf man was Roddy Fenton. He'd worn the same gruesome mask when he'd gone trick-or-treating last Halloween. The only difference now was that he was wearing a bigger size sweat suit and his voice was deep instead of high and crackly. As I said, Roddy had grown a lot in the past year.

I rang the doorbell, and it was opened almost immediately by Robert in a tremendous, baggy, white clown's outfit with a high ruffled collar and black pompoms down the front. He was wearing a pointy-topped white clown's hat, also with pompoms, but no mask because, after all, there was no way Robert could have hidden his identity behind a little black mask.

Robert was the perfect host.

"Oh, I'm delighted to see you," he beamed at us, "whoever you are."

Robert reached for my cape, and I gave it to him. I still hadn't uttered a word. I didn't want my voice to give me away.

"You're gorgeous!" Robert hissed in my ear. "But who's that with you?"

Had Robert guessed who I was? I'd set my hair in big, big rollers and sprayed it with hair stiffening lotion so it would look softly waved. But maybe it was crinkling up again anyhow. That would be a dead giveaway. Cautiously I felt it. No, it seemed to be holding the set.

I shrugged at Robert to indicate I didn't know who my partner was. Both Robert and the wolf man, I noticed, were looking at me with curiosity and intense interest.

"Hey," Roddy, the wolf man suddenly exclaimed, "you're not Cathanne. Your hair isn't as red as hers. It's more blond. I couldn't tell outside in the dark. Gee, I'm sorry if . . ."

I put my hand on Roddy's arm and smiled with my luscious hot-pink lips. As the old Glenda, I was still

mad at Roddy from our last encounter. But tonight I
wasn't really that Glenda. I was a mysterious, masked,
dance-hall queen whom Roddy didn't recognize. And
somehow I didn't feel like *me* at all.

Gently, I nudged Roddy past Robert toward the
center of the big living room where seven or eight kids
were standing around in costumes and masks. The
party was just beginning and hadn't warmed up yet.

Some of the disguises were real puzzlers, but of
course I had no trouble spotting Mary Lou with her
candle and her blood-spotted hands and Patty with her
gauzy dress and a lopsided wreath of flowers on her
head. Roddy and I walked right up to them, and I
looked straight at them wondering if they'd know me.
But all they said was, "Oh, look at the wolf man. That
must be Roddy," because they, too, had seen him out
trick-or-treating last year.

As for me, they just stared. And then Mary Lou said,
"Who could *you* be? You don't look like anybody in
our English class."

Roddy grabbed my arm. "She's with me. We're
crashing." He put his finger on his fangs. "Uh, don't
say anything."

Mary Lou and Patty both giggled under their masks.
But they seemed to believe that I was a stranger who
had come to the party with Roddy. Everything was
turning out marvelously. People really didn't know who
I was. Yet I could feel their admiring glances and hear
them whispering about my beautiful costume behind
my back.

Robert came over and placed a heavy hand on my
shoulder.

"Listen," he said, breathing heavily, "could I borrow

you for a moment? I've just got to show you to my mother."

I nodded, still not wanting to speak a word. As we left the room, Robert called out to the others, "Hey kids there's punch and there's lots of stuff to eat in the dining room. And the music's playing. So start dancing."

Robert had taken my hand and led me through a wide hallway into a wood-paneled den with lots of warm, tweed-covered furniture. So far I thought his house was the nicest I'd ever seen in Havenhurst.

Robert's parents were sitting in front of the TV set. As soon as Robert's father saw me, he got to his feet. He must have been about six feet four and had a very large frame that was well padded. Then his mother stood up. She was very tall and well padded, too. But she wasn't blubbery like Robert; she was statuesque.

"Who's *this?*" Robert's mother asked, looking very impressed. "Oh, I'll bet this costume wins a prize when your teacher gets here."

Robert grinned. "Mom, Dad, this is Glenda."

I stared at Robert with real disappointment. "How did you know?" I asked. "Everybody else seems to be stumped. Roddy, Patty, Mary Lou—none of them recognized me."

Robert smiled mysteriously. "I'd always know."

His parents smiled too, as though they were in on the secret.

"Let me see," Robert's father said, carefully taking in the details of my costume, "I'd say you were supposed to be a saloon entertainer from one of the popular TV westerns."

"I'm a dance-hall queen," I said quickly, fingering the pink feather boa at my throat. "No special one."

Robert was staring at me hard. "You certainly are," he said, "a queen."

I could feel my cheeks getting hot. It was embarrassing and even smothering to have all three Frys standing and eyeing me this way. Sure I liked being admired. It was a whole new experience for me after a lifetime of feeling klutzy and fat. But it was a little too much all at once.

I glanced around nervously. "Maybe," I said, "we'd better get back to the party."

Robert snapped to attention. "Sure," he said.

I smiled to his parents, and they both sat down. We started for the living room, which had suddenly gotten a whole lot noisier. It seemed like a bunch of new kids had just arrived.

"Don't worry," Robert whispered sharply into my ear as we entered the living room. "I won't give away your secret, Glenda."

I stood there and shuddered for an instant. Robert's breath was so steamy-hot it had given me the chills.

There *was* a whole bunch of newly arrived kids in the living room. But the one who seemed to be causing the most noise and attracting the most attention was Cathanne. She wasn't even wearing a mask. I guess she figured that in the costume she was wearing she'd be recognized instantly anyway.

Cathanne was dressed as a chorus girl. She had on the shortest shorts I'd ever seen, made out of blue velvet, a tight sleeveless silver lamé blouse, and a shiny silver top hat worn at a rakish angle. Her long red hair hung down in back. She had on blue mesh tights that made her long legs look even more shapely and slender than they were and silver tap-dancing shoes. I noticed with dismay that she, too, was wearing blue eye makeup. And I think she had on false eyelashes. She looked sensational.

Everybody was exclaiming over her outfit, especially those really skimpy shorts.

"Aren't you freezing?" Mary Lou in her flannel Lady Macbeth nightgown wanted to know. "You didn't even wear a coat."

Cathanne laughed. "So what? The heater was on in the car." She looked around the room excitedly. "Is he here yet?" she asked in a husky whisper.

Roddy advanced toward Cathanne in his wolf man mask. "Yeah, I'm here Cathanne. Gee, if I'd waited like you told me to I'd have been standing outside in the cold all this time. Lucky for me some other gorgeous woman came along and I went in with her." Roddy urged me forward to show me off to Cathanne.

"Oh," Cathanne said to Roddy, "I didn't mean whether *you* were here yet, although I am sorry about being so late. You *know* who I mean. I mean Mr. Hartley . . ." Cathanne stopped short as I drew closer. "Who's this? Say, I *like* your costume." She fingered the curling feathers of my boa. "I always wanted one of those. Where'd you get it?"

I just smiled and raised one shoulder. By now almost everyone in the room was crowding around Cathanne and me, examining both our costumes from all angles.

"She won't say who she is. She won't say anything," Roddy volunteered. "It's been like that all evening. She's a mystery guest."

"Oh, but that's not fair," Cathanne said. "I'm not wearing a mask."

"Yes, but you should be," Patty under her lopsided Ophelia wreath pointed out. "When Mr. Hartley starts choosing the prizewinners, he's not supposed to know who they are."

"That's right," Mary Lou agreed.

"Nonsense," Cathanne snapped. "I know who both of you are even though you're wearing masks. In fact, I know who just about everybody in this room is. Do you think Mr. Hartley's so dumb he isn't going to be able to tell?"

"All right, then," Roddy challenged Cathanne, pressing his shoulder hard against mine. "If you're so smart, who is *she?* We'd all like to know."

Cathanne shrugged. "She's probably not even in our English class."

A voice suddenly boomed out from the edge of the crowd.

"Oh, yes, she is."

Could that have been Robert after his promise not to give away my secret?

Cathanne looked annoyed. She stared straight at me. "Then either say something or take off your mask."

I shook my head in refusal.

"Don't talk!" a few of the kids advised. "Make her guess."

"No fair!" some others called out. "Say something. Anything."

But I just didn't feel like giving up yet. I'd worked so hard to fool them all. I'd struggled through all those weeks of dieting so that now, in my glamorous costume, I didn't look anything *like* fat Glenda anymore.

I stared straight back at Cathanne, and all I did was smile, hoping my hot-pink lipstick wasn't all eaten off by now.

"Oh, really," Cathanne declared impatiently. "If you *are* somebody in our English class, I want to know who you are!"

And with that, Cathanne's arm shot out in the direction of my face and her long fingers grabbed for my mask.

14

I saw Cathanne's hand diving toward me and I reached up to try to stop her. But I was too late.

With a single strong tug, Cathanne had pulled the black sequined mask clear up over my head. She stood with it in her raised hand and gaped at me, while I groped wildly to fix my hair.

"Oh, I don't believe it!" she cried. "You look so . . . different." Her fingers brushed the beauty mark that I'd put on, even though it had been hidden under my mask all this time. "That's fake, isn't it?" Cathanne asked, as if trying to reassure herself. Her eyes probed my face and body some more. "It's *really* Glenda."

All around me there was a chorus of amazed voices. "Glenda . . . Glenda . . . it's Glenda." I was sure that somewhere on the fringe of the group I heard somebody say, ". . . fat Glenda, only she doesn't look fat. How come?"

"Oh, my goodness!" Patty squealed, standing directly

in front of me, holding both hands to her cheeks. "All this time I've been saying to Mary Lou, 'Why is she so late, when is she going to show up?' I never *guessed* this was you!"

"Patty was beginning to think you weren't coming to the party at all," Mary Lou explained. "She said you'd been having so much trouble trying to think of a costume, maybe you'd just given up."

Now that the suspense was over, everybody began taking off their masks. Roddy tugged at his wolf man's head. Underneath, his face was red and sweaty. "Wow," he said, wiping his forehead with the edge of his sweat suit sleeve, "you sure had me fooled, Glenda. For a while there I actually thought you were Cathanne. And *she's* skinny."

"Oh, well," I replied, "that was outside in the dark."

"Still," Roddy insisted, "just look at you." He paused and his face seemed to get even redder. "Now you don't *honestly* think I'd ever have called you 'Jelly Belly,' do you?"

"Maybe you did and maybe you didn't," I remarked half-seriously.

Roddy gave me a look as if to say, "Don't let's start *that* again," and immediately changed the subject. "Gee," he exclaimed, looking around the room, "I guess I *am* the only kid here who's not in your English class. Cathanne invited me just for a joke. She said who'd know if I wore a disguise? But then she stood me up by getting here real late. She's crazy."

I didn't say anything even though I was pretty angry at Cathanne myself. I was examining my mask to make sure she hadn't torn it when she ripped it off.

Just then the music came to a sudden stop, and

Robert appeared in the middle of the room waving his arms wildly.

"Quick," he called out, "everybody get your masks back on. You, too, Cathanne. He's here!"

There were shouts and whistles, and Cathanne shrieked, "He's here? But I haven't *got* a mask."

Robert, the perfect host, coolly handed her a plain black eye mask from a bunch he was holding. Then he put one on himself. He looked around, a billowing black and white clown. "Okay, let's keep it quiet. See if he can guess who we are. Ssshh, everybody. Ssshh."

With exaggerated steps, Robert tiptoed to the front door. He must have been watching out the window for Mr. Hartley's approach because it wasn't until Robert's hand was on the doorknob that the bell actually rang.

My heart began pounding. Everybody was standing very still. And they, too, seemed to be charged with tension. I could hear a few suppressed nervous giggles from the girls and choked whispers from the boys.

With a fancy bow Robert threw open the door and exclaimed, "Welcome, Mr. Hartley!"

There was another moment of suspense, and then in the door frame stood David Hartley looking even more handsome than I'd ever seen him in class. He was wearing a ribbed white turtleneck and a dark blue jacket. His eyes were sparkling and his lips were smiling.

Oh, how long will it take till he sees me, I wondered? And will he recognize me?

But at that moment Mr. Hartley wasn't looking directly into the room at his masqueraded English-class students. His attention seemed to be directed elsewhere. He was reaching behind him. For something.

Or someone. And a second later, her hand clinging to his, a young woman walked into the room at his side.

She had long, thick honey-blond hair, perfect cheekbones, and a dazzling smile. She had to be either a very glamorous actress or a very high-salaried model. And I was pretty sure she was also Mr. Hartley's girl friend.

"What of it?" Mary Lou was saying about twenty minutes later, as we were drinking fizzy red punch ladled from the big bowl on the dining room table. "So what if he wants to bring one of his lady friends to the party? He's single and he must have scads of exquisite creatures like her in his life. I don't see what everybody's so upset about."

"We're *not* upset," Patty retorted, her eyes flashing. "We're just surprised is all. We didn't expect it. Though, as you say, maybe we should have. I guess she was his date for the evening, so they just naturally stopped by at the party together. What do you think, Glenda?"

I nodded in agreement, my mouth full of a cream cheese sandwich with olives and pimientos in it. Then I took a long sip of the sugary red punch. What was I eating all these fattening little party sandwiches for, all of a sudden? I wasn't hungry. And the punch was actually making me sick to my stomach.

"What I can't believe," Patty went on, "is that she's real flesh and blood. She's . . . she's so perfect. She seems nice, though, doesn't she? I mean when he introduced her around. Do you think he's in love with her? Maybe they're only friends." Patty leaned closer so Mary Lou couldn't hear. "Maybe she's just an actress he knows from his Broadway days. Remember what Miss Esme told us, Glenda?"

Mary Lou edged nearer. "If you're whispering about Cathanne, you can say it out loud. Did you see her face when he came in the room with *her?* My, didn't Cath look upset, though."

I stuffed another party sandwich into my mouth. Even though it was liverwurst, which I hated, I swallowed it anyway. In the living room, David Hartley and his date, who had been introduced to us as Nina—no second name—were having "just one dance" before the costume-judging began. Most of the kids were standing around mesmerized, watching the stylish jerks, tilts, and twists of David and Nina's shoulders, heads, and hips. No question about it, they were both terrific dancers.

"Glenda," Patty said, suddenly looking at me with a deep concern, "your lipstick's gotten awfully smeary. You ought to fix it."

I snapped to attention. What was the matter with me? Was I the old Glenda, eating myself silly, or the new one? I had to try to concentrate. I went to the closet where Robert had hung my cape, took my makeup kit out of the pocket, and headed for the bathroom. Luckily it was empty. I took off my mask and looked into the mirror. On the outside anyway, I was definitely the new Glenda. All I needed was a little fresh hot-pink lip liner and filler.

When I went back into the living room feeling a lot more confident, David and Nina were sitting side by side on the couch like a king and queen. They had white note pads on their laps and the kids were all gathered at one end of the room ready to parade before the two judges one by one. Robert's mother and father had come in from the den to watch the contest.

"Over here!" Patty hissed, and I dashed across the room to wriggle into a tiny space between her and Mary Lou. Robert was going around asking each of us what or who we were supposed to be, so he could announce us to David as we walked past.

"It's like being in a fashion show," Patty whispered. "Oh, I feel so nervous."

"Or like a cattle show," Mary Lou muttered. "I just know *I'm* not going to win a blue ribbon."

"Oh, don't be so negative," Patty scolded her.

Robert finished taking down the names of our costumes and explained to us that David and Nina were going to judge us on "originality, effectiveness, and execution of costume," scoring each of the three on a point basis of one to five. The kids with the most points would win first, second, and third prize.

Mr. Hartley clapped his hands and rubbed them together. "Are we ready? Who's first?"

"Ready," Robert replied.

"Shoot," David said. And he glanced at Nina and winked as if to say, "See how much fun this is going to be." On the other hand, that wink could have meant, "Don't worry, this'll be over in a jiffy and then we'll get out of here fast." I had the feeling that Nina wasn't exactly delighted to have been brought to the party.

Mary Lou was one of the first to go.

"Lady Macbeth!" Robert announced in a voice about five times louder than it needed to be. "In the sleep-walking scene."

There went Mary Lou, her blood-spotted hands shaking and her candle, which Robert had lit for her at the last moment, flickering madly.

There was a big round of applause as she safely

made it to the other side of the room, and David and Nina began jotting things down on their pads. They were supposed to make independent decisions, but I saw Nina take a very quick sidelong glance at David's pad. I have to admit I didn't like Nina very much. She was exactly the kind of person, I decided, who'd sneak a look at somebody else's paper during a final exam.

"Next," David called out. And so it went. I was anxious to get my part over with, but a lot of kids pushed ahead of me. In pressing past me, Cathanne gave me a sharp poke with her elbow. *Maybe* it was an accident. I'd never seen her as high-strung as tonight. You could tell she was determined to get a prize.

As soon as Robert announced her, Cathanne started across the room expertly twirling a cane and walking with a chorus girl strut. Then, when she'd gone halfway, she stopped directly in front of David and broke into a two minute tap-dance routine. She got a big hand for that, and David and Nina scribbled furiously on their pads before calling for the next person.

I was almost last. My cheeks were hot and my mouth was dry. My legs felt wobbly and I was scared of tripping in my high curvy heels.

"A dance-hall queen!" Robert bellowed.

For an instant I couldn't seem to move at all, and then a voice hissed in my ear, "Go on, Glenda, do your stuff. You're gonna win!" It was Roddy.

His words seemed to electrify me. If Cathanne could put on a great big act, why couldn't I? I flung the end of my hot-pink feather boa around my neck, stuck my hands on my black taffeta hips, and strutted across the floor with a swinging gait.

I could hear all sorts of appreciative noises coming

from the watching kids. Under the disguise of my costume and mask, I was beginning to feel really bold, so much so that when I got in front of David and Nina I stopped and did something that surprised even me. I unwound the feather boa from my neck and, just as Sally Langridge had done, I dropped it to my hips, pulled it tight, and did a quick little shimmy followed by a bump.

There was stomping and whistling. A girl actually screamed. Then I sashayed off to the other side of the room. It was over. What a relief! At that moment I felt so good I didn't care if I'd won or lost.

The last few kids followed, and then David and Nina went off to the den to add up their scores. We all took our masks off. It was nearly eleven o'clock, and Robert's mother started serving cups of cocoa and cutting a big chocolate cake decorated with orange and chocolate icing. I watched Patty stuffing a wedge of cake in her mouth, but I had lost my appetite completely. I couldn't eat a thing.

"What's taking them so *long?*" Mary Lou fusssed. "I'm supposed to be picked up for home along about now."

Just then David and Nina reappeared. Nina already had her coat on. Mr. Hartley raised one arm and said, "Sorry this is going to have to be so brief, but we're going to have to rush away as soon as I announce the winners. The actual prizes will be given out later, not tonight. Sorry about that, too." He gave us all a winning smile to make up for the disappointment.

David held up one of the white score pads. "Here goes . . . the final and irrevocable decision of the judges . . . starting with third prize. For exceptional

117

imagination in dreaming up a fine character costume, and hoping you succeed in getting the blood off your hands, third prize goes to . . . Lady Macbeth!"

Mary Lou nearly keeled over, and the next thing she did was to grab hold of me and start shouting to everyone in a thin, screeching voice, "It was Glenda's idea. Honest. She thought of the whole thing!"

I had all I could do to unwind Mary Lou's skinny white arms from around my neck. She was practically hysterical. There was lots of applause, and I saw Mary Lou's nose and eyes redden as if she were about to cry.

Second prize went to Andy Garr, a boy in our English class who had worked out a really ingenious Tin Man costume from *The Wizard of Oz* made out of cardboard and heavy aluminum foil. Poor Andy had barely been able to move all evening because of his stiff costume and big head mask, so everybody was really glad that he'd won.

"And now," Mr. Hartley announced, as Nina began to glance impatiently toward the door, "for first prize . . ." Mr. Hartley reached out and took Nina's hand. "Nina and I really want to thank you for your patience because that was a tough one. We agonized and we soul-searched and there was no other fair way to do it. For first prize, there was a tie. So . . . we have two winners, both charmers, both beauties, and both talented. Yup, you guessed it, kids . . . the chorus girl *and* the dance-hall queen!"

Cathanne gave an almost blood-curdling scream, and then she did a strange thing. She ran straight for David Hartley, threw her arms around his neck, and kissed him smack on the mouth.

I saw Mr. Hartley stagger with surprise and saw the shock register on Nina's face. But Mr. Hartley hadn't been an actor for nothing. He recovered quickly. "A kiss for *all* the winning females," he proclaimed, holding out his arms. "Glenda, Mary Lou, where are you?"

I grabbed Mary Lou by the shoulders and pushed her forward until she was directly in front of Mr. Hartley. She didn't put her arms around his neck, though, as Cathanne had done. She didn't kiss Mr. Hartley either. She just put her cheek alongside his mouth and let him brush it with his lips.

Then Mr. Hartley turned to me, holding his arms wide. I hesitated for a moment and then ran into them. His lips touched mine in a warm silken kiss. Blissfully, I closed my eyes. I was sure, in that moment, that I would love David Hartley for the rest of my life.

15

As they say in show business, after a triumph like that, what do you do for an encore?

Well, of course, I couldn't just rest on my laurels. I had still more pounds to lose for the really big moment, the time when I would audition for a dancing part in Mr. Hartley's show.

Patty, just as she'd said she would, kept after Miss Esme about helping us prepare a dance number for the tryouts, and now we were putting in rehearsal time at the studio three days a week.

"I have to warn you," Miss Esme had said, when she first started teaching us the movements, "that this is my own choreography. It's a combination of free-form dance and exercise rhythms. It's not standard Broadway stuff, and it may not be David Hartley's cup of tea."

After we'd watched ourselves in the studio mirror

a couple of times, Patty and I told Miss Esme we liked it, and it *was* easy to do.

"Good," she said. "I think it suits you two well because instead of stressing the differences in your sizes it shadows and blends the two figures." We were "big" and "little." No matter how much weight I lost, I would always be taller and broader than Patty.

After Mary Lou had won third prize for her Lady Macbeth costume at the Halloween party, I was almost sure that Patty would be jealous and annoyed with me. She never had liked the Ophelia costume much. But, to my surprise, Patty and I were now better friends than ever. She had been sincerely happy that I'd won first prize and she was especially glad that I'd tied her old friend Cathanne.

"The way Cathanne's been acting lately," Patty had remarked bitterly, "everyone is going to start hating her. And did you see the face she made when she found out what the prizes were going to be? What did she expect Mr. Hartley to give her—a pair of diamond earrings?"

We'd learned just before the party ended that night that the prizes were going to be books and that Mr. Hartley was going to select a special one for each winner. That was why he hadn't been able to choose them in advance. I wondered what my book would be. As long as Mr. Hartley wrote something in it, I didn't care what it was. I would treasure it always.

In the days following the party, Patty had started questioning me about what it had been like to be kissed by Mr. Hartley. I made a joke out of it because I wanted to keep my feelings very private, so I said, "Why don't you ask Mary Lou? Or Cathanne?"

But Patty had burst out laughing and said, "Mary Lou didn't get kissed on the mouth. And Cathanne went smacking into *him*. Come on, Glenda, you were the only one he really kissed."

Just hearing Patty say that made me shudder with delight. I'd been so afraid that I'd die of embarrassment the first time I saw Mr. Hartley after the party. But he was so normal and natural and funny in class the next Monday that I soon relaxed. I did feel warmer and closer to him than ever, though, and I was so happy when he gave me a batch of seventh-grade exam papers to mark.

But Patty just wouldn't let up. "Did you tell your mother your English teacher kissed you on the mouth?" she wanted to know.

I hadn't of course. Even though there had been plenty of witnesses, including Robert Fry's mother and father, it just wasn't something you went home and told your mother.

I got out of giving Patty a direct answer by saying, "What would *you* do?" and Patty had just giggled.

"You do like him a lot, though, don't you, Glenda?"

"Doesn't everyone?"

"Yes, but he likes you back. I can tell. That makes a difference."

There was no way, of course, to stop Patty from telling Miss Esme all about the party. Patty said she had to find out who Nina was and maybe Miss Esme would know.

Miss Esme listened in her quiet way while Patty described the costumes we wore and who the winners were. She seemed truly interested. But when it came to Nina, Miss Esme shook her head.

"She could have been anybody, an actress or a model, as you say. A casual friend or a close one. I really don't know anything about David Hartley's private life. He's an attractive man so it's only natural that women flock to him."

"I think," Patty said, glancing at me slyly, "that Nina *is* his girl friend. All the time they were at the party I had the feeling she was anxious to get away. Didn't you, Glenda?"

I nodded in agreement.

"And when the kissing started, she really looked sort of mad."

Miss Esme raised an eyebrow. "Oh? What kissing was that?"

Patty looked at me apologetically. "It's okay, isn't it, Glenda, if we tell Miss Esme about his kissing the girls?"

I began to redden. But already Patty had begun to describe breathlessly how Cathanne, who was very brazen and had this big crush on Mr. Hartley and was sure to get into his show, had rushed into his arms after having tied with me for first prize.

"So then he kissed Glenda, too," Patty added. "But he *really* kissed her. On the mouth. And that Nina woman looked even madder than when Cathanne kissed him."

"Did she?" I asked with interest. I hadn't been able to see Nina's face at the time, of course.

Miss Esme took a very deep breath. You could see her whole chest cage rise beneath her leotard. "Well, as I said before, Nina may be one of many, or she may be 'the one.' I have to tell you, though, that

David is something of a lady-killer and he can also be a 'user.' "

I must have been frowning at what Miss Esme was saying. She looked at me very seriously. "I realize you girls probably like him a lot. At your age it's pretty natural, you know, to feel some kind of puppy love. A while back it used to be movie actors mostly. Then it got to be rock stars. Sometimes it's a 'real' person, someone you see on a daily basis. You're so happy to be near him that you're practically willing to be his slave."

Was Miss Esme some kind of clairvoyant? Did she know about all the papers I'd been marking for Mr. Hartley?

"I don't see what's wrong with that," I blurted out defensively.

"Nothing's wrong with it," Miss Esme replied, her cool dark eyes looking straight into mine. "Just so long as you don't expect too much in return. The person with a case of puppy love wants to give, give, give. And the love object—the rock star or whatever—just *is*. He could turn away anytime without giving you a second thought. That's why puppy love is a one-way street. Or you might even say a dead-end."

My cheeks felt as though they'd caught fire. I looked away from Miss Esme into Patty's wide, staring eyes.

"So be careful, Glenda," I heard Miss Esme say in a faraway voice that seemed to be coming to me through a thick fog of sound. "I mean it for your own good. Just be careful."

A couple of weeks later at three-thirty in the afternoon I was sitting next to Mr. Hartley in the school auditorium. On my lap lay a large-size note pad. It was the first day of auditions for the school show, and Mr. Hartley had asked me if I would like to be his secretary or, as he had put it, his "girl Friday."

My job consisted of getting the names, classes, addresses, and telephone numbers of the dozens of kids who would be trying out all through the week. I was supposed to put down a short but clear description of each act that was performed—singing, dancing, juggling, magic, comedy skit, or whatever—so Mr. Hartley could recall it easily. I was also supposed to time each act so he'd know how long it was likely to run if he used it in the show.

"Are you sure you can put in this many hours after school?" Mr. Hartley asked me with a concerned glance as we settled into two seats in the fifth row center. "Sure you'll be able to get your homework done for all your other classes?"

I nodded. "Of course."

Actually, I would be missing Miss Esme's Tuesday and Thursday dancercise classes that week, and I'd have to find a little extra time somehow to rehearse our own dance number, the one that Patty and I were going to do. We were scheduled to go on on Friday, the last day of tryouts, and Miss Esme had promised to come watch the audition.

"Oh, good," Patty had said, after Miss Esme had agreed to be present. "At last you'll be able to renew your acquaintance with David Hartley. Who knows? He might even ask you to help with the show. You know, coach the dance numbers."

I'd seen Miss Esme stiffen.

Later I'd told Patty, "That was a dumb thing to say

to her. Number one, I don't think she likes him very much. And secondly, she's a professional person, and you know this is a school show for which nobody gets paid."

"Okay, okay," Patty had answered. "I just thought it would be nice if old friends got together. But, as you say, maybe they're not. Old friends, that is."

The week of tryouts was hard work, but I loved every minute of it. There were so many kids who wanted to audition for the show that most afternoons Mr. Hartley and I stayed in the auditorium very late. With the days so short that time of year, I usually found myself walking home from school in the dark.

Cathanne tried out on the second day, and she did a really sensational jazz-and-tap routine wearing an outfit similar to the one she'd worn to the Halloween party. It was no surprise that she was so good. Everyone had expected right from the start that she'd be getting into the show.

Some of the other acts I watched that week were great, some were just fair, and a lot of them were really terrible. I kept feeling more and more hopeful about our dance number, even though Patty kept grumbling that we needed more rehearsal time than we were getting.

One reason I was glad that we weren't auditioning until Friday was that I had actually been losing a little more weight each day. Partly, I suppose, it was my "girl Friday" chores, which included a lot of running up and back to the teachers' room during the tryouts to get Mr. Hartley fresh cups of hot coffee. He drank lots and lots of coffee and he always wanted it hotter than it was. But mostly I think it was just being around

126

David Hartley so much that had me shedding weight faster and faster.

How could Miss Esme say that puppy love, as she called it, was a one-way street? Maybe I *was* giving Mr. Hartley a whole lot of time and work. But look what he was giving me. Since the first time I'd laid eyes on him back in September, I'd lost eighteen pounds. The "thin me" inside was really clawing her way out now. And it never would have happened if not for the fact that I so desperately wanted to be thin for him and for the show.

Friday came at last. Patty and I had decided to audition in plain black leotards, and I had bought a brand new one. Can you imagine me, once a mass of bumps and bulges and sausagelike rolls of fat, feeling good enough about myself to let Mr. Hartley see me in a leotard? Oh, I wasn't skinny exactly, but I was firm all over now and really well-proportioned.

Miss Esme arrived at the school around four o'clock. Patty, who was waiting for her at the back of the auditorium, brought her over to meet David. Of course, I'd already told him that our "dancercise" teacher knew him, and he'd acted really pleasantly surprised and said he was anxious to see her again.

Now they were meeting in Havenhurst—"a long way from Broadway," as Miss Esme had put it—for the very first time. If there were any strained feelings between them, you'd never have known it from the way David behaved. As soon as he saw Miss Esme coming down the aisle of the auditorium, he lunged out of his seat, raced to meet her, and gave her a great big bear hug.

"Esme!" he said warmly. "Where've you been keeping yourself? The girls told me you were in town. We should have gotten together sooner than this."

Miss Esme, who was much, much shorter than David, looked up at him calmly. "My studio's right over on Main Street, David. I've been there since September. Exactly as long as you've been teaching here at the school."

David just kept smiling down at her, his eyes sparkling.

"Shouldn't we go and get ready to do our number?" Patty asked breathlessly.

"Yes," Miss Esme agreed. "You'd better. I can't stay long."

I got up to leave. Mr. Hartley made a mock-sad face at Patty. "You mean you're taking my Glenda away?" He turned to Miss Esme. "It's no joke. Glenda's my good right arm. She's been keeping data sheets on the tryouts. She keeps me in hot coffee. She's incredibly efficient at everything."

Miss Esme placed her hand lightly on Mr. Hartley's arm. "Don't worry, David. You'll survive. You always have."

Then she called after Patty and me, "Break a leg!"

That's show business talk for good luck. I don't know why. It sounds just the opposite, doesn't it?

16

A week had gone by. Every day at school people came up to me asking if the show had been cast yet. And after school, kids I didn't even know called me up on the telephone. They all figured that since I'd been Mr. Hartley's secretary during the tryouts I'd be the first to know which acts he had decided to put in the show.

But, of course, I didn't know anything. Mr. Hartley had taken the data sheets from me late on Friday afternoon and said he would "mull them over" on the weekend. But when Monday came, he confessed to me that he'd spent the weekend with friends in New York City and hadn't had a chance to even open his brief-case.

Patty kept pestering me each day. "Ask him. Ask him about *us*."

"I can't," I told her, even though I was feeling pretty optimistic about our number. "I'd be embarrassed.

He'll announce the casting to everybody when he's ready."

"I think he should tell you first. After all, you're not just anybody. Look how hard you worked for him all last week. He owes you something." Patty clutched my wrist. "We *were* good, weren't we, Glenda? Miss Esme said we did well. Oh, I hope he thought so."

Even Cathanne started hanging around me.

"I know what everyone's been asking you and I'm not going to ask you *that,* Glenda. All I want to know is *how* is he going to announce the casting. Should we expect a postcard or a phone call or what?"

Cathanne's question seemed like one I could ask Mr. Hartley without sounding too anxious about myself.

"You know," he said, looking thoughtful and stroking his jaw, "I haven't really thought about that. Do you have any suggestions, Glenda?"

I loved it when he asked my advice. It made me feel he was treating me as a grown-up woman, a person he not only liked but respected. How *could* Miss Esme say David was a "user," or that he was as selfish and indifferent as some glorified rock star?

I *had* been thinking about the best way to announce the casting, so I slowly replied, "I think a good way would be to put all the names on the school bulletin board. Then everybody would find out at one time. It wouldn't be fair if some kids got a phone call or a postcard and others had to wait and wonder if they were still going to be notified."

Mr. Hartley snapped his fingers. "Gotcha! Ah, Glenda," he added softly, "what would I ever do without you?"

I was dying to add that, of course, if he *wanted* to

tell me anything about *our* dance number right now he could. I'd have sworn to keep it a secret, even from Patty.

But I just couldn't get the words out, and meantime Mr. Hartley was assuring me that he was definitely going to look through the tryout sheets on the coming weekend and he "might even have the cast list ready by next Monday or Tuesday."

Another whole weekend to hold my breath! I couldn't help looking a little disappointed. "But . . . but everyone's so anxious. They keep asking *me*. And I don't even know about myself . . ."

Mr. Hartley patted my shoulder. "Not to worry," he said in a soft teasing singsong. "Not to worry."

What did that mean? Did it mean not to worry because he was going to announce the casting of the show for *sure* next week? Or did it mean not to worry because I definitely *was* going to be in the show?

The following Monday, just before class, Mr. Hartley asked me if I could come and see him in the English room at three o'clock, right after school ended.

"Sure," I replied.

"I need to go over one or two of the tryout sheets with you," he added. "A couple of facts I'm fuzzy about. Maybe you can refresh my memory."

"Sure," I repeated, practically bouncing out of my seat.

"Until three then," he whispered. "And remember, mum's the word."

The rest of the day was torture. Everybody seemed to sense that something was up. Patty was a nervous wreck by now, and I was trying to avoid her as much as possible. Cathanne had actually taken to trailing around after me and had even apologized to me for the way she'd practically torn off my mask at the Halloween party. "I was just so anxious to see who was inside that terrific costume," she'd explained.

The only people who still seemed to be behaving normally were Mary Lou, who hadn't tried out for the show at all, and Robert, who hadn't tried out either but was going to be working on the lights for Mr. Hartley.

It felt like the school day would never end. Today, today, I kept telling myself; today is THE DAY. Surely the dance number that Patty and I had done would be in Mr. Hartley's show. It was original, it was funny, the music was catchy, and Miss Esme had said that we performed it well.

Patty had tried very hard to find out from Miss Esme if David had said anything to her when they were sitting together watching us audition. But Miss Esme either refused to be pumped or had honestly not been able to tell if David liked it or not.

"I didn't see your competition, the other dance entries," she'd explained to Patty and me, "so I can't even say how you rated. As to David's response, he smiled all the time and he applauded hard. But I've noticed he always does. So that doesn't *mean* anything. He might as well have been deadpan."

"Let's face it," I said to Patty later. "She really doesn't like him. She's always putting him down, sort of."

"Probably she's just trying to keep us guessing," Patty remarked hopefully, "so the thrill will be even greater when we find out we're in. Oh, Glenda, we *will* get in the show! I just know it. What fun."

Dodging Patty and everybody else that Monday after school wasn't easy. I said I had to go to the science room to finish my experiment and I actually puttered around there until the hallways were clear. Then I dashed down the corridor to the English room.

Mr. Hartley was sitting at hs desk studying a long scribbled sheet of ruled yellow paper. He looked up with a slightly worn expression when I came in.

"Too much talent," he muttered. "A director's nightmare. Believe me."

I just smiled at him.

"Sit down, Glenda," he said, pointing to a chair drawn up alongside his desk. "I'm serious. I think TV is what's done it. Kids today absorb performing techniques—timing, stage presence, a sense for comedy—with their baby formulas." He ran his pencil up and down the ruled yellow sheet. "There was so much good stuff presented. Some nice original skits, some great song-and-dance numbers. I needed a balance, though. It was a real juggling act."

Mr. Hartley pushed one of the data sheets from the tryouts toward me. "Can you cue me in on this one? Those three ninth-grade girls, the singing act. What were they wearing?"

"Tee shirts," I replied, "that said 'Baby Doll.' "

"Oh, yes," he said quickly. He took back the sheet. "I remember now. The caterwaulers. We can forget about them."

Mr. Hartley scratched his head. He had taken off his jacket and had opened his shirt at the neck. I loved being close to him when he was working and thinking hard. It made me feel very special.

Suddenly Mr. Hartley tossed his pencil down on the

desk and leaned back. He clasped his hands behind his head and stared at the ceiling.

"Callbacks," he said, as though he were thinking out loud. "I hate having callbacks. It makes the kids nervous. It gets their hopes up, and then if they don't make it the second time they feel doubly rejected. No, I want to make all the final decisions now."

He sat up straight again and took a last intent look at the cast list in front of him. "This is it then, Glenda. Would you make a nice clean copy of it right now, *if* you can understand my miserable handwriting. I'll post it on the bulletin board before we leave today."

Mr. Hartley shoved the scrawled yellow sheet directly in front of me, and I pounced on it with all ten fingers. At once I began reading the names of the kids Mr. Hartley had picked to be in the show. My eye ran down the page and up again.

David Hartley's handwriting *was* hard to read. But as carefully as I looked, there was no Glenda Waite on the list. Patty wasn't on it either. But Cathanne was. Her name was very near the top of the list.

A strange crawly feeling came over me. I actually began to itch all over. Surely Mr. Hartley had made a mistake. He had simply failed to put my name down because it was understood—without any formalities at all—that I would have a part in the show.

I could hear Mr. Hartley rattling and rearranging papers at my side. I didn't dare look up. I couldn't think of anything to say. Suppose I asked him my question and the answer really was no?

"Whoa!" Mr. Hartley's voice suddenly broke through my uneasy thoughts. His hand, with its beautiful square-cut nails, was drawing the sheet of paper away from me. "What's the matter with *me?* That list's not complete. I've got two more names to add."

My itching stopped almost instantly. A lovely feeling of warm relief swept over me. Just as I thought, Mr. Hartley had omitted our names, Patty's and mine, by accident. I got up from the chair and went and stood behind him, watching closely over his shoulder. What difference did it make now if he knew how anxious I was? I *was* going to be in the show and that was all that mattered.

Yet, as I watched Mr. Hartley writing down the last two names, my peculiar itchiness crept back bit by bit.

"That's it," he said cheerfully, passing the sheet to me over his head. "You can start copying." He began jamming the rest of the papers on his desk into his briefcase.

"But . . . but *these* two names . . ." I blurted out, looking down at them in disbelief. My voice was hoarse and cracked.

"What about them?" Mr. Hartley asked absently.

I moved around in front of his desk extending the list toward him.

"Wasn't . . . wasn't *I* supposed to be on here? You know, the . . . the dance number Patty and I did."

Mr. Hartley's eyes looked directly into mine.

"Why no, Glenda," he answered, looking somewhat surprised. "I didn't think you were too serious about that. I thought you were just trying out for the fun of it. Besides, there's something else I'm going to ask you to do in the show. Something, believe me, that's much, *much* more important."

"Like what?" I asked jumpily.

He grinned triumphantly. "Well," he said, giving me

a long, teasing look, "like being the assistant director."
He paused. "Now, how's that grab you?"

I tried to swallow the lump in my throat. "You
mean," I said, seeing very clearly that he didn't mean
for me to have a performing part, "being your . . .
assistant."

He nodded. "Call it what you like. Glenda, you'll be
the person who pulls it all together. You'll be scheduling rehearsal times, keeping stage notes, handling liai-
son with lights, props, costumes, publicity. It's an
exciting job." David's eyes, which had faded to an
almost slate blue a few moments before, became their
dazzling brilliant color once again.

He leaned toward me across his desk.

"Glenda, it wouldn't be fair to tear you apart with
this assistant director stint *and* a dance number, which
incidentally I think needs some work and improvement.
I know I've already asked a lot from you. And you've
given generously. But I'm hoping you'll say yes to this
job because it means a very great deal to me. Will you
say yes, Glenda?"

I stared at him numbly. This wasn't what I'd wanted
at all. I'd worked so terribly hard to lose weight, to
become trim and firm, and to look good dancing in
front of an audience. And I'd thought Mr. Hartley
would have noticed this and realized how much it
meant to me.

Yet even as I gazed at him in deep disappointment, I
could feel David Hartley's electricity working on me. If
I said no to the assistant director job, what then? I'd lose
my only chance to be connected with the show, to be
close to David, closer even than I'd ever expected.

I swallowed hard again and, even before my faint

nod, David read the answer in my eyes. He jumped to his feet.

"Wonderful!"

He rubbed his hands together like someone with a hearty appetite about to dig into a sumptuous meal. "We'll begin rehearsals right after Thanksgiving."

17

Later that Monday afternoon the cast list went up on the school bulletin board, and by 8:45 on Tuesday morning a thick cluster of kids was crowded around it finding out who was in the show and who wasn't.

There were screams of pleasure and groans of disappointment. I didn't hang around there very long. In fact, as soon as I saw Patty approaching the group, I darted into the girls' bathroom nearby.

Of course, she found me there, standing worriedly in front of the mirror and aimlessly tugging at my hair with a comb.

"You!" she said, pausing dramatically in the doorway, her finger pointed at me and her eyes practically shooting sparks. "You traitor."

Wordlessly, I placed a curled hand against my chest. What did she mean by that?

Patty advanced on me. "You knew about this last night, of course. You *wrote* that list. But you didn't call me to tell me, did you? That makes you a coward as well, Glenda!"

"It . . . it wouldn't have been fair," I stammered. "Everybody was supposed to be notified at the same time."

"Baloney," Patty stormed. "The real reason you didn't tell me was that you knew it was your fault we didn't get the part."

"My fault. How? Listen, don't you think I feel terrible about it, too? Did you forget all about my dieting and exercise, and practicing that dance number over and over?"

"We didn't practice nearly enough," she retorted angrily. "I kept telling you we needed more rehearsals. But no, you had to be Mr. Hartley's secretary, his little goody-goody all that time during tryout week when we should have been rehearsing."

I shook my head. "I don't think it would have made any difference. There were other dance numbers he liked better."

"That's *not* the reason." Patty disagreed. "Would you like to know the real reason?"

"Well, what is it then?" I challenged.

"Simple." Patty laughed bitterly. "You and he had it all cooked up that you were going to be his assistant on the show. I just now saw your name written in small letters at the bottom of the casting announcement: Glenda Waite—Assistant Director. So who do you think you're fooling? You knew all along our dance number didn't stand a chance."

"That's a lie!" I shouted. "I never knew till yesterday afternoon. I . . . I felt like crying when I saw our names weren't on the cast list. And when I asked him about us, he said he had this other job for me. I just didn't know what to do at first. Honestly, Patty, that's the way it happened."

Patty looked away disgustedly. "I should never, never have teamed up with you. I should have done the number by myself. I'd be in the show now instead of being . . . dumped."

"I'm not so sure you would," I remarked. "He did say the dance number needed some . . . improvement. I think he meant in the choreography. And you don't have to feel 'dumped.' You can still be in the show. You can work on the costumes or the props or the publicity. Lots of jobs are open. You could even work with Robert Fry if you wanted to. He's going to be doing the lights."

Patty gazed at me grumpily. "Thanks a lot."

I looked at both our images in the mirror over the sink. "I just don't think you should be a sore loser. Everybody can't be in the show. There's nothing disgraceful about taking a backstage job. In fact, I'm sure it's going to be lots of fun."

"For you, maybe," Patty remarked. Her eyes narrowed. "I'm beginning to think Miss Esme was right about you."

I didn't like Patty's look. "And just what do you mean by that?"

"I mean that you're nothing but a groveling slave for David Hartley." Patty caught my reflection in the mirror and waggled a finger at it. "You just better remember, Glenda, what Miss Esme said. She warned you, you know, to be careful."

*   *   *

The long Thanksgiving weekend arrived after only one more day of school, during which I noticed that Patty didn't seem to be talking to me.

More and more I thought of Sara, who was still my best friend and surely now my only friend, and on the Friday evening after the holiday I decided to write her a letter. Sara had been with me through thick and thin—in the truest sense. She'd been so happy about my weight loss and about my winning costume at the Halloween party that she'd actually written me a poem about it:

> Hail to Glenda,
>   The dance-hall queen
> Who captured first prize
> On Halloween!

Now I had to write Sara my not-so-happy news about *not* getting into Mr. Hartley's show.

Just as I was about to start, my mother came into my room gnawing on a turkey leg left over from yesterday's big Thanksgiving dinner.

"Would you like a snack, dear?" she asked. "I was just slicing up some of the turkey meat and rearranging things in the refrigerator." She waved the turkey leg at me guiltily. "Well, you know how it is. Anyhow turkey meat is very lean. It's one of the least fattening things you can eat. Oh, and there's some delicious apple pie left."

My mother was at it, as usual, walking around the house in the evening, eating and serving snacks.

"You didn't have any dessert at dinner yesterday," she reminded me, "even though it was Thanksgiving, a

141

special day. You really should taste that pie, Glenda, before it's all gone. I just gave your father some, warmed and with a scoop of butter pecan ice cream on top."

I looked up. A small voice inside me seemed to say, "Why not?" After all, I wasn't in training anymore to look great for Mr. Hartley in my new black leotard. One little piece of pie. After what I'd been through in the past few days, it didn't seem like such a sin.

"Okay," I murmured. "Just this once."

My mother returned with the pie, bringing a slightly smaller piece for herself, and she sat down to share the snack with me.

I looked at the creamy, melting glaze of ice cream. A large pecan half, just ripe for the picking, was embedded in the top of the scoop.

"You gave me too much," I said softly.

"Oh, nonsense," my mother urged. "Treat yourself for once. You haven't been looking very happy for the last couple of days, Glenda. I don't think so much self-denial is good for the soul."

I took a forkful of the warm, juicy pie with its crisp, buttery crust. "You don't understand," I said, with my mouth full. "If I started eating this way even once in a while I'd gain weight in no time. I'm going to have to stay on my diet for the rest of my life."

My mother looked stricken. "Oh, no. What a thing to say! Surely you could expand it a little, make an exception now and then."

I shook my head. "Uh-uh. I have to lose even more weight, not gain any back." I looked down suddenly at my quickly emptying plate. I'd already finished nearly all the pie and ice cream, and I could easily have eaten more. "And you're a bad influence," I added.

Before my mother could reply, the phone rang and she got up to answer it. She was back in a moment.

"For you," she said, "and you're going to be surprised. It's a young man. And he has the nicest voice."

Did my mother mean a "young man" like Mr. Hartley, or what? Of course, it was ridiculous to even think that David Hartley would ever call me up. But then again you could never tell. After all I was the assistant director of his show, and we were supposed to begin rehearsals right after Thanksgiving. Maybe he had some special instructions for me.

I went to the phone with my heart thumping.

"Hello," I said very cautiously, in case my voice sounded quavery or too eager.

"Hello, Glenda," the voice came back. "I guess you're surprised to hear from me."

"Uh, I'm not sure," I said, trying hard to place the voice. "I don't know who this is."

"You don't? I thought that would be very easy for you. It's Robert."

Fat Robert! I didn't say the words out loud, of course. All I said was, "Oh," in a flat kind of way.

Robert didn't seem at all put off by that. He cleared his throat. "Well, first of all I wanted to say congratulations."

"Congratulations?" I repeated. "On what?"

"On being made assistant director to Mr. Hartley. You know that's a very responsible job, Glenda."

"Yes," I said, "very."

"I'm going to be working backstage also," Robert

143

added. "On the lights and the carpentry for the sets and stuff like that."

"Yes, I heard."

"So we'll be seeing quite a lot of each other."

"Yes, I guess so."

"Of course, I'm sorry you didn't get a dancing part. I heard you were very good at the tryouts."

"Who told you that?" I asked with a little more enthusiasm. I wondered if Mr. Hartley might have said something.

"Gosh," Robert replied, "I can't remember exactly."

I couldn't help thinking what a really dumb conversation we were having.

More throat clearing from Robert and then, "Well, anyway, Glenda, being it's a holiday weekend and all, I thought maybe you'd like to . . . to . . ." Cough, cough. "That is, I wondered if you'd like to go to the roller rink with me tomorrow. My treat, of course."

I gulped. Was Robert actually asking me out on a date?

"Um . . . is anyone else going skating?"

"Oh, sure," Robert chuckled, "a whole bunch of people will be there, I guess. But I'm just asking you."

I remembered how envious Patty and Mary Lou and I had been about Cathanne's date at the roller rink with that mysterious ninth-grade boy. I'd imagined myself, slender enough some day to look almost as graceful as Cathanne, skating there with some unknown boy who had asked me for a date. And the image had stuck in my mind.

Now, only a few months later, it was actually happening to me. And yet, the picture was all wrong. I just couldn't see myself turning up at the roller rink with fat Robert lumbering along beside me. Probably I was cruel to think of him that way. But I hadn't lost all that weight to get asked out on my very first date by the fattest boy in the entire school!

I wondered, too, if Robert would have asked me out if I'd gotten a dancing part in the show. Did he feel more comfortable about asking me because, like him, I was going to be one of Mr. Hartley's backstage crew? I had to think of an answer quickly.

"Robert," I blurted out, "I'm . . . very sorry. But I'm going to be . . . going away with my family for the entire Thanksgiving weekend."

Robert sounded surprised. "But, Glenda, this *is* the Thanksgiving weekend."

"I know," I stumbled, "but . . . but we're getting a late start."

"Oh, too bad." Robert sighed gently with disappointment. "But never mind, Glenda. I'll get you another time."

I crossed my fingers. I hoped not.

The moment I was off the phone, shaking a little from nervousness and frustration, I headed straight for the kitchen to get another scoop of butter pecan ice cream and to see if there was any apple pie left.

18

What a day I was having! Mr. Hartley's show was already three weeks into rehearsal, and I'd spent my entire study-hall period running around school trying to set up a place to rehearse that afternoon. Mr. Hartley preferred the auditorium, but when he couldn't get that he usually tried for the gym or even the lunchroom.

Today it turned out we couldn't have the auditorium because it was the last week before Christmas and the choral society was using it for practice. So in desperation I went to the custodian's office to see if we could have the gym.

Mr. Hauser, the custodian, eyed me sourly through his steel-rimmed spectacles.

"Nope," he said. "You go back and tell that dramatics teacher of yours that he can't have the gym. It's being used for basketball practice. He knows that, so why's he even asking?"

I leaned forward anxiously. "Well, then, what about the lunchroom?"

"Dang it, no!" Mr. Hauser said, lightly slapping the surface of his desk. "I got enough trouble with the lunchroom staff as it is. They don't want that place messed up once it's all scrubbed and tidied for the day."

"Oh, but we wouldn't mess it up," I assured him. "There'd be no eating or anything like that. It's just to have a run-through of a few of the dance numbers."

Cathanne and some of the other dancers were supposed to come and work on their routines that afternoon because David had some ideas for improving them. As for eating, there *would* be David's coffee, which I had to keep bringing him freshly made and scalding hot during the rehearsals. But I didn't have to tell Mr. Hauser that.

My job as assistant director had turned out to be much harder than the "girl Friday" job I'd had during tryout week. Not only did I have to scrounge around for rehearsal space, but I had to notify the cast members when and where to show up, keep all the notes David kept dictating to me, and follow up on all sorts of unexpected and knotty problems that were probably going to keep cropping up for months, until we finally put the show on in the spring.

Mr. Hauser got up from his desk and rubbed his hands together.

"Listen, girlie," he said, "no offense meant, but why don't you go and tell Mr. Hartley to take these things up with the teachers directly in charge? And tell him to do it himself. Why's he sending a kid like you around on these errands, hmmm?"

"Be . . . because he's busy teaching classes, for one," I replied. "And because I happen to be the assistant director of the show, for another."

Mr. Hauser's thin lips stretched into a smile. "Oh, fancy title. And what about you? Shouldn't *you* be busy *attending* classes?" Mr. Hauser leaned forward across his desk. "Look, miss," he said, not unkindly. "Mr. Hartley's new in the school and maybe he doesn't know the ropes yet. I'm not saying this rehearsal scheduling can't be worked out. But it's gonna take a lot of trouble-shooting and, like I said, it's not a kid-size job."

I left Mr. Hauser's office red-faced with embarrassment and anger. I didn't like the things he'd said about Mr. Hartley and, even worse, I still hadn't managed to get a place for us to hold the rehearsal that afternoon. The dancers in the cast were going to meet in the auditorium at three o'clock, and they were going to be pretty disappointed when they got there. I was already late for my science class, so I didn't even have time to report the bad news to David.

During science I had trouble concentrating on protozoan life forms because I was trying hard to think of how I could surprise David with some big new, wonderful rehearsal space. I even thought of Miss Esme's studio. But, of course, she held her own classes there in the afternoons.

Today, as I had for the past couple of weeks, I would again have to miss my dancercise class because of my job on the show. Patty, who was talking to me again but in a cool, stilted way, had said, "Well, if that's your choice, Glenda. But you're missing some really good exercise sessions."

"I'll make them up," I assured Patty. I had already explained to Miss Esme about my absences, and she'd said I could come to the classes that I missed in the spring term when I had more time.

"It won't be the same, though," Patty said dryly. "Besides, you shouldn't suddenly stop your exercising. You're going to lose all the muscle tone that you worked so hard to build up."

I had simply shrugged. But deep down I had a feeling Patty was right. I wasn't jogging much anymore either, partly because it got dark out so early and partly because I had to use most of my extra time catching up on my homework. Worst of all, though, I had begun eating more—desserts and snacks and bigger portions of everything!

Looking back I could see pretty clearly that all my eating troubles seemed to date from around Thanksgiving time—not getting a dancing part in Mr. Hartley's show, my fight with Patty, and then that phone call from fat Robert asking me to go to the roller rink with him.

All I could think of was the poem Sara had written for me a long time ago and how true it was still:

> *Every time*
> *You take a beating,*
> *You try to make it up*
> > *By eating.*

After my last class ended that day, I went to my locker to get the clipboard and notes that I carried to rehearsals. As I was hurrying through the crowded school corridor on my way to the auditorium, I ran almost head-on into Roddy Fenton.

"Hey," he exclaimed, holding up his hands in mock self-protection, "it's Glenda, the dance-hall queen. Long time no see. Where you running to?"

"Oh, sorry," I gasped. "I didn't see you. I'm late for rehearsal. Mr. Hartley's show, you know. He's waiting for me."

But Roddy didn't seem to grasp the idea that I was in a hurry. He leaned against the wall as if he had all the time in the world and was expecting me to stand there and chat with him.

"Oh, yeah?" he said with a lopsided grin. "What part do you have?"

"None," I replied. "I'm the assistant to the director. Listen, Roddy, I have to go. The rehearsal's supposed to start right away."

"Oh, really? Say, could I come and watch?"

I hesitated. "Well . . . actually the rehearsals are supposed to be just for people involved in the show. But everything's so mixed up today anyway . . ."

I started down the staircase with Roddy at my side jumping double steps.

"Who got parts?" Roddy wanted to know.

"Oh, lots of kids. Cathanne, of course. Gee, where have you been? I thought everybody in the school knew about the show."

Roddy shrugged. "Not too interested, I guess."

I wondered then why Roddy wanted to go to the rehearsal with me. But I didn't stop to ask him.

By the time we got to the auditorium, the choral society was grouped on the stage going through the opening bars of "A Partridge in a Pear Tree." I didn't see Mr. Hartley there or any of the kids from the cast.

"See," I said half-scoldingly to Roddy, "I told you I was late. They probably all got disgusted and left."

I walked up to the front of the auditorium and asked a few kids who were hanging around in the first few rows if they'd seen Mr. Hartley. They all shook their heads and turned away.

Finally one kid sitting way over at the other end of the row piped up. "Yeah. Mr. Dixon said he and his kids could use the music room." Mr. Dixon, who was the teacher in charge of the choral society, was up on the stage directing the singing.

"Come on," I said to Roddy with an urgent wave of my hand. "They're in the music room up on the second floor."

"Gee, calm down, Glenda," Roddy said, following me at a leisurely pace. "What's this guy Hartley gonna do if you're late? Make you take a salary cut?"

"Not funny, Roddy," I said over my shoulder as I rushed up the staircase, my clipboard resting on top of my armful of school books.

Roddy caught my elbow. "Hey, wait a minute," he said. "At least gimme some of those books you're carrying before you have a stroke."

I stopped and gratefully unloaded most of my school books into Roddy's arms.

"Thanks," I panted, starting for the next step.

But Roddy didn't budge. "Come on, Glenda. Relax. What ever happened to that dance-hall queen at the Halloween party? Say, remember when you put on your act with that pink feather thing in front of Hartley and his girl friend? That shimmy you did and that bump?" Roddy exploded into a loud but appreciative laugh. "Now that was what I call relaxed."

"I remember," I said, thinking back wistfully. "But Halloween was a long time ago. It's Christmas next week. You heard them 'partridging' down there in the auditorium."

"So what? You're still the same person. Or are you?"

That was a good question. "Listen, Roddy," I tried to explain, "that was a party and I was wearing a costume and a mask. It was easy to be somebody else that night." I frowned. "Maybe I'd feel a *little* like that now if I'd gotten a part in the show."

"But you didn't," Roddy remarked, watching my face carefully. "So you took this cruddy job instead, and it's driving you nuts. Why don't you quit?"

I looked at him in bewildered shock. "I . . . I promised."

"Aw, come on." Roddy's eyes hadn't left my face.

"Listen," I said uneasily, "you don't understand. So why are we standing here arguing? Or whatever it is we're doing."

I bounded up the rest of the steps to the second-floor landing. Part way down the corridor, from the open doorway of the music room, I could hear the steady rhythmic sound of footwork and a man's voice calling out in time to the cadence.

152

I hurried toward the sound. The music room had a small stage, most of it taken up by a grand piano. The seats were arranged in a semicircle that sloped upward toward the rear and there were two doorways, one at either end of the bottom row of seats.

Roddy and I entered by the first doorway we came to. A few kids from the cast, who had dancing parts, were scattered among the seats, their eyes intent on the stage. I followed their gaze. The piano had been pushed back and a space cleared for dancing. There were two dancers on the stage, their backs to Roddy and me. One of them was Cathanne, her red hair piled on top of her head. The other one was Mr. Hartley. He was in shirtsleeves and, at that moment, he was dancing in unison with Cathanne, his left arm encircling her waist and their hands locked at Cathanne's midriff.

Softly, with Roddy following at a short distance behind, I mounted the steps to the third row of seats and began to work my way around to center stage. Mr. Hartley didn't see me at first. Both he and Cathanne had their heads down, looking at their feet and counting steps.

When they stopped dancing and David finally looked up for a moment, he stared right through me making no sign or gesture.

His attention was completely on Cathanne. "Now," he said, bending his head to hers, "let's try this segment again. From the top."

I watched them, fascinated.

"He's *good*," Roddy whispered from the next seat. "And they're very good together. What a team!"

"I know," I said. The routine they were practicing was quite different from the one Cathanne had danced at tryouts. David must have taught her a set of entirely new steps and movements. And she seemed to have picked them up instantly and to be following his instructions expertly.

Finally their practice session came to an end. I left my seat and rushed up onto the stage to speak to David.

"I'm sorry I was late," I said quickly, "and I'm awfully sorry I didn't have a chance to tell you about not being able to get the auditorium for this afternoon. I tried real hard to get the gym or the lunchroom, but Mr. Hauser said . . ."

Mr. Hartley cut me off with a wave of his arm. "Forget it," he said, sounding slightly out of breath from the dancing. "I sent most of the kids who turned up this afternoon home. Been working out mainly with Cathanne today. Kid has terrific talent."

"Yes," I agreed. "She has."

"I could use some coffee," he panted. "Think you can rustle me up some?"

"I . . . I don't know," I said. The teacher's room where I made Mr. Hartley's coffee was down on the main floor and sometimes, this late in the afternoon, it was locked. "I might need the key."

Mr. Hartley searched in his pockets. "Darn, must have left it somewhere. Listen, see what you can do, Glenda. Maybe it's open. And make sure it's hot." He grinned and spelled out the word for emphasis. "H-O-T."

I started obediently on my errand.

"Oh," he called out after me, "and after that you can go home. Won't need you anymore today."

I turned. "What about the rest of the week? Mr. Hauser says that you should . . ."

"Forget about it," he answered abruptly. "I've decided I'll work out with Cathanne and some of the other kids in here for the rest of the week. That'll take us through to Christmas vacation."

Cathanne, who had been standing off at a little distance, leaning down from the stage and talking to one of the other kids, overheard and came rushing over to David. "Oh," she screamed, "do you mean that! Really?"

Before David could answer, Cathanne, delirious with joy, leaped off the ground and threw her arms around David's neck.

Stunned and horrified, I watched him untangle himself. At least she hadn't managed to kiss him, as she had on Halloween. But David didn't seem particularly upset. In fact, he appeared to be smiling at her in fond amusement.

I suddenly felt myself filled with annoyance with David and brimming with hatred for Cathanne. Maybe I'd disliked her all along but had always tried to hide my feelings because I'd truly admired her looks and talent.

Behind me I heard a strange hissing sound, like steam escaping. I turned and saw Roddy standing just behind me. He wasn't looking at me, though, or even at Cathanne or Mr. Hartley. He was staring at the ceiling with an exasperated expression on his face. Maybe he, too, had really had it with Cathanne and the way she was behaving.

My cheeks were burning. In a quavering voice I heard myself speaking to Mr. Hartley. "But," I said teasingly, trying not to sound as angry as I was, "if

I'm not going to be here for the rest of the week, who's going to bring you your hot, hot coffee, David? . . . spelled H–O–T!"

It was the very first time I'd ever used Mr. Hartley's first name to his face. But I didn't care.

Mr. Hartley drew his brows together in baffled irritation. I'd never seen this expression on his face before. It didn't make him look indignant, though; he just looked grumpy and hurt, almost like a little kid.

"Hey," he began softly. "What's all *this* about?"

But before he could say anything else, Cathanne had drawn herself up beside him, boldly and possessively.

" 'David'? Well, well," she remarked. "Aren't we getting pretty familiar?"

I could have smacked her. *"You* should talk!"

"Yeah," Roddy brayed in a cracking voice.

Cathanne ignored Roddy and took a step forward, placing herself almost directly in front of Mr. Hartley, as if she were trying to protect him. "Listen," she said, her eyes glittering, "what are you getting so hot under the collar about, Glenda? I should think you'd welcome a little time off. And if you're worried about . . ." She turned to gaze up briefly at Mr. Hartley, ". . . 'David's' coffee, calm down. There'll always be *somebody* around to make it."

"Sure," I agreed, giving her what I hoped was a searing look. "Maybe he can even teach you!"

I turned and ran off the stage. My books and my jacket were at my seat a few rows up. I wanted to get them and get out of there as quickly as possible.

Roddy grabbed my arm. "Where're you going? I've got all your stuff right here."

I didn't even bother to say "Good!" I snatched at my

jacket and headed straight for the doorway, with Roddy chasing behind me.

"Glenda!" Mr. Hartley called out.

I froze. Should I pretend I hadn't heard him? Should I turn or not?

I turned. He was standing on the stage, alone now. He looked very tall, even though he was slouching slightly, his hands thrust into his trouser pockets.

"We'll talk about the after-Christmas schedule, you and I. Okay?"

I thought he sounded a little sheepish. Was his promising to talk about the rehearsal schedule supposed to thrill me after everything that had happened this afternoon?

I nodded dumbly and left.

"Whew!" Roddy said, as soon as we were out in the hall. "Whew!"

I rushed on ahead of him down the stairs to the first floor, made a sharp turn to the right, and marched down the corridor toward the main office. Two doors beyond it was the door to the teacher's room.

I stopped directly in front of it. Then, very slowly, I turned the knob. The door opened. The room was empty except for a slightly startled man teacher who looked up from a pipe he was lighting.

Roddy peered into the room over my shoulder.

"Hey, Glenda, you're not . . ."

"Not what?"

"You're *not* going to make that guy a cup of coffee?"

I looked at Roddy, but I didn't answer.

"Well, it's a fair question," he insisted. "Why'd you open the door, huh? Just answer me that."

Still silently eyeing Roddy, I thrust my arms into the

sleeves of my jacket and zipped it up in one swift continuous motion. Then I reached over and took my books out of Roddy's arms.

"Oh, just to make sure I *could* have made him coffee if I'd wanted to. That's all. Any more dumb questions?"

Roddy broke into a broad grin. "Nope."

19

Even though I begged her not to, my mother baked Christmas cookies in the days just before the holiday. She assured me, as she always did, that she was only making them to give away as gifts. And, as always, she and I nibbled and sampled and *ate* far too many.

I knew that if I went on like this I'd soon be on my way to weighing as much as I had *last* Christmas. And yet I couldn't seem to stop myself. I was certain now that David Hartley had never even noticed if I was fat or thin. In fact, he had probably never seen me at all except as a good-natured lackey, somebody to be there when he needed her and not get in his way when he didn't.

If only he'd stopped Cathanne when she'd lashed out at me. But instead he'd actually let her act as his mouthpiece, hardly saying a word, maybe even finding it secretly amusing that two of his students were having a fight over him.

As far as talking with Mr. Hartley about the after-Christmas rehearsal schedule, I just assumed he meant we'd do that *after* Christmas. For the rest of that week, I sat in my front row seat in English, did my classwork, and rushed out of the room each day the moment the bell rang. After a few uncertain glances in my direction, Mr. Hartley let me do as I pleased, probably figuring—the way grownups usually do—that I'd "get over" it.

But now that I knew David didn't care, I couldn't seem to care anymore either. Already my clothes were getting tight. I stopped tucking my shirts into my jeans and had begun wearing them on the outside, leaving the top button of my pants open.

"Everyone puts on a little weight during the holidays," my mother consoled me, when I showed her what was happening to me. "You'll make a New Year's resolution and take it all off in January. You'll see."

I shook my head miserably. "I won't," I said. "I'll just be fat again. Fat forever. Forever fat." Like you, I thought, watching my mother, whose figure looked like a stuffed-to-bursting sausage as she bustled around the kitchen arranging her trays of walnut crescents and butter stars, double-chocolate drops, and frosted spice bars.

Suddenly two large fat tears began to roll down my cheeks.

"Oh, my goodness!" my mother said, rushing to my side. "What's wrong?"

Everything, I thought, as a cascade began to gush from my eyes and nose. Everything! And in a fit of watery rage I reached over, grabbed a chocolate-glazed log cookie and crammed it into my mouth. Before I had even swallowed it, I stuffed in a date-and-nut chew. I began to circle the kitchen like a wild animal on the prowl. I ate a fat, buttery Santa Claus decorated with white icing and candied cherries. I ate a Christmas-tree sugar cookie with red and green sprinkles. I ate an entire gingerbread man with pink-frosted eyes. I downed two still-warm pecan lace cookies and gobbled up a dripping tablespoonful of chocolate glaze.

"Oh, help!" my mother screamed in a hoarse voice, even though there was nobody within hearing and the windows were all shut tight. She grabbed me around the waist. "Glenda dear, please stop. Please, please, please."

My mouth was stuck together with chocolate glaze. I couldn't speak.

"Water," I heard my mother saying in desperation. She sat me down hard on one of the kitchen chairs and brought a brimming glass. "Here, drink this. It'll probably make you throw up. But it's better than getting sick."

I pushed the glass away from me. "No . . . don't want to . . . throw up. Want to . . . get fat. Fat, fat, FAT!" I extended my arms far apart and blew air into my cheeks to puff them up. "Want to be the fattest girl in the world, fatter than fat Robert, fatter than the fat lady in the circus. Four hundred pounds . . . no, six hundred. More . . ."

"Glenda, oh, Glenda." My mother was standing in front of me wringing her hands. "Please stop. You're frightening me to death. Not that I haven't heard of people who've been dieting going on sudden eating binges. But this is *too* much."

"That's it," I shrieked, pointing hysterically at my mother.

"What? What is? I don't know what you're talking about."

"What you just said. There's a *fat* me inside, don't you see? A fat Glenda inside a thinner Glenda that wants to come out and be fat again."

My mother pulled up a chair and collapsed into it wearily. She wiped her forehead. "I don't understand. When you were fat, you used to say there was a *thin* you inside that was trying to get out. Now make up your mind. Which is it?"

I dissolved under a fresh onslaught of tears. When I was smaller, I'd always cried the "wettest" of any kid around. My father used to call it "turning on the waterworks."

"Now, listen," my mother suggested gently after my outburst had subsided a little, "why don't you go and write a letter to Sara? That always seems to calm you down and make you feel better."

I was surprised. My mother had never seemed to care much for my writing to Sara and she'd certainly never encouraged it before.

I buried my head in my arms. "Even Sara," I moaned, "wouldn't be able to help."

I had never written Sara that letter at Thanksgiving time. I had merely sent her a Christmas card on which I'd scribbled that a letter would be coming soon. But what could I possibly write her now? How could I tell her that all her good advice, her sincere and loving help and understanding had been for nothing, that I was once more on the road to Blubbersville!

*   *   *

During Christmas week, Miss Esme gave a party at the dance studio. She invited all her students and said they could bring along a friend or a parent if they wanted to.

At first I wasn't going to go because I was so ashamed of how fat I was getting. But Patty kept urging me and said she had invited Mary Lou, who wouldn't know anybody else at the party. My mother kept coaxing me to go, too, so I finally I went.

Miss Esme seemed glad to see me and she asked me how Mr. Hartley's show was coming along.

"Oh, just fine," I said, trying to sound breezy and confident.

"I'm sorry the dance number you and Patty did wasn't picked," she said, her eyes searching my face. "I warned you both that it mightn't be his cup of tea."

I shrugged. "Oh, I don't think it was that. I guess we . . . that is, I just wasn't good enough. I always *think* I can dance, but I guess I don't look very good doing it."

"Not true," Miss Esme said with a serious expression. "I checked you out and, believe me, you looked fine."

I broke into a smile. Somehow I knew she wouldn't lie.

Miss Esme's expert eye gave me a quick once-over. "You've gained a little weight since I saw you at the audition, haven't you?"

I blushed and nodded. "More than a little. I . . . I don't get much time for exercising."

Miss Esme didn't comment. "Enjoy the party," she said pleasantly. Then she excused herself and walked away.

Although there were refreshments—healthful and natural ones like fruit juices and brown-bread sandwiches and crunchy oatmeal cookies—I was much too self-conscious about the weight I'd gained to eat anything under Miss Esme's eyes.

I sat with Mary Lou to watch the entertainment, which included an advanced dancercise demonstration with Patty in the front row of performers.

"My, that looks hard," Mary Lou whispered.

"Oh, it's not," I assured her. "Even I can do it. Well . . . could. I guess you noticed I've put back a little weight." I figured it was better for me to say it before Mary Lou did.

"I didn't notice really," she replied. "But I'm sure you can take it off again. I do so admire your will power, Glenda."

The subject of my vanished will power was so painful that I couldn't even reply.

A little later on I went over to the refreshment table with Mary Lou so she could get herself a small paper cup of apple juice. "So what have you been doing with yourself this week?" I asked her. "Have you seen Cathanne?"

Mary Lou raised her eyebrows in surprise. "Cathanne? Why she's off to New York City for the Christmas vacation. I thought you knew."

"No, I didn't. What's she doing *there?*"

Mary Lou took a tiny sip of juice. "Well, from what I heard she's seeing about 'advancing her career.' She's supposed to sign up for lessons at one of those professional dance studios in Manhatttan and then travel in every weekend. She's got an aunt who lives in the city."

"Hmmm," I pondered uneasily. "How'd she ever come up with that idea?"

"Oh, I heard it's not altogether hers. It seems Mr. Hartley suggested it. He told her she'll never get any proper training for the theater in this little hick town." Mary Lou lowered her voice to a hush and glanced around the room for Miss Esme as she spoke the last few words.

"Oh," was all I could think of to say. Various pictures began to leap through my mind—Cathanne and David dancing together at the rehearsal in the music room, Cathanne dancing at a professional studio while David looked on admiringly, Cathanne on the stage in a Broadway show that was being directed by David.

"Of course, she's so crazy about him," Mary Lou hissed in my ear, "that she'd always take his advice. I wonder if *he* likes her. I don't know. I thought he had more sense. What do you think?"

I looked straight ahead of me as I spoke. "If he *can* like somebody like her," I said, trying to hide the choking despair in my voice, "then I'm . . . well, sort of disappointed in him."

"Oh, me too," Mary Lou agreed. "And not only because Cathanne is such a vain, selfish, self-centered person. I'm also disappointed in him because I found out he doesn't keep his promises." Mary Lou nudged a little closer. "Do you remember that he said all the kids whose costumes won at the Halloween party were going to get books as prizes?"

I nodded.

"Did you ever get your book, Glenda?"

I shook my head. "No. Although I did hear him say

he was working on it. Something about trying to pick out the right book for each person . . ."

Mary Lou looked doubtful. "Oh, well," she commented, looking across the room, "you're the assistant director on his show and all, so I guess you still have faith in him. I just hope you're right."

When the studio party ended, I went over to say good-by to Miss Esme. She took my hand in hers, which was surprisingly warm and soft.

"I know how busy you are these days with your job on the show, Glenda. But try to come to some of the dancercise classes or at least to Saturday morning jogging. You're always welcome, you know."

I nodded. "I'll try."

"And," she went on, not letting go of my hand, "if there's anything you would like to discuss with me at any time, about your weight, or any other problem . . . anything . . ."

"Th . . . thanks," I said, trying hard to swallow the rising lump in my throat.

"You know," Miss Esme added, her eyes smiling faintly, "you might *think* there's a fat girl inside you trying to get out. But you can just as easily think like a thin girl, which you've already proved you could become." Her eyes darkened. "It's all up to you."

She let go my hand, but her eyes still held mine as though trying hard to transmit an important message.

I knew then, of course, that my mother had talked to her about my hysterical pre-Christmas cookie-eating binge.

20

"So how was your Christmas vacation?"

Fat Robert had appeared out of a side street and caught up with me on my way to school the first morning back. He must have been running because he was breathing especially hard.

"It was okay," I said dully, thinking of how much weight I'd gained in a mere ten days. Soon I'd be looking like a perfect twin for fat Robert. So how could I blame him for not losing any weight?

"I had a great vacation," Robert announced cheerfully. "Went to Florida to visit my grandparents."

I looked at Robert. His fair, rosy complexion was redder than usual, but I'd thought at first it was because of the cold weather and the fact that he'd been running. I wondered if he was that same tomato-red color all over his body and tried to imagine what he must have looked like in his bathing trunks. The picture I got made me shudder.

"That's how come I didn't phone you during the holiday," Robert went on, as he lumbered along beside me. "You know, maybe we could have gotten together like we tried to during Thanksgiving. Only that time *you* went away."

For an instant I couldn't figure out what Robert meant. Then I remembered the lie I'd told him and quickly said, "Oh . . . right."

"How's the show doing?" Robert wanted to know. "I'd like to get a look at the lighting situation in the auditorium. Did you book any rehearsal time in there this week?"

"Nope," I replied in a flat voice.

"You didn't?" Robert sounded surprised. "I thought that was your job."

"Was," I told him, "is correct. From now on it's Mr. Hartley's. The custodian says he's supposed to handle that himself."

Robert slowed near the entrance to the schoolyard. "Wow! You had me worried there for a minute, Glenda. I was afraid you were going to say you were quitting or something. You know I'm really looking forward to working with you as a member of the crew." Robert stopped and leaned against the tall iron gate. "Uh . . . and there's something else I've been wanting to mention, too." He looked very serious. "I . . . I've been discussing you with my mother."

I stared at him uncomfortably.

"Discussing *me?*"

"Yup. You remember you met my mother and father at the Halloween party?"

"Yes?"

"Well," Robert said, clearing his throat, "uh, don't be offended at this, Glenda, but I was telling them how you had been kind of, ummm, fat at the beginning of the term and how much weight you'd lost in only a couple of months. Then they saw for themselves how great you looked at the party."

I turned my head away. "I know. But I don't want to talk about weight now, Robert. I'm gaining it all back. Can't you tell?"

Robert shook his head. "No. I can't."

"Well, that's only because I'm all bundled up in a heavy jacket and stuff."

Robert positioned himself directly in front of me. A sly smile lit his face. "I guess you can't tell that *I'm* losing weight."

"Losing weight?" I shook my head. "To be perfectly honest, Robert, I can't."

Robert kept on looking delighted. "I guess not. Not yet, anyway. But I am. Eight pounds so far, Glenda. *Eight* pounds. I started around Thanksgiving time. Not bad, huh?"

"No," I said. "That's very good. What made you do it?"

"You did," Robert replied, aiming a finger at me.

"Oh, come on," I said, waving his finger aside. "I did not."

"No, you really did. You were my inspiration, Glenda. So then my mother took me to the doctor, and he put me on a new diet and exercise program, and this time I'm really following it. Of course, I've got plenty to lose, more than you ever did. Also, he says I'll never be a real lightweight. It's just not in my genes."

169

I nodded, recalling how tall and big-boned both of Robert's parents were.

"But at least," Robert continued, "I won't be a quivering mountain of flesh. Let's face it. I guess . . . well, nobody likes going around with a fatty." Robert peered at me more closely. "For example, *you'd* like me better if I were thinner, wouldn't you? Be honest, Glenda."

I began to laugh, not at Robert but at us. "You know, Robert," I said, suddenly realizing that I felt very relaxed with him, just as I would with any good friend, "this is very funny. *You're* losing weight on account of me, and I'm gaining weight on account of . . . of . . ."

Robert stood by patiently, waiting for me to finish.

"Oh," I said disgustedly, "on account of I'm stupid!"

How could I tell him the real reason? On account of David Hartley, I would have had to say. On account of he was *my* inspiration. And now . . . now he's not.

I felt so awkward about seeing Mr. Hartley for the first time since before Christmas vacation that I actually considered cutting my English class. But what good would that do? I had English five days a week.

I entered the classroom a little bit late. Patty and Mary Lou were already in their seats and so was Robert. In a moment or two Cathanne came in, walking with a new, self-assured swagger. She looked different, too, older and more sophisticated. I noticed she'd had her hair cut into bangs. A thick fringe rested low on her forehead and the rest of her hair had been

170

trimmed a little shorter all around. She bent down to talk to one of the girls who formed a special group of her admirers. The second bell rang.

"Hey," somebody yelled out, "where's teach?"

Cathanne raised her head. "Calm down. He's coming."

"She oughta know," somebody murmured.

I shifted uncomfortably in my seat. Did everyone know that Cathanne had spent Christmas week in New York City? Had she seen David there? How close were they really?

Suddenly David walked into the room with ringing footsteps. He tossed his briefcase onto the desk, smiled at the class, his teeth appearing a more dazzling white than ever, and rubbed his hands together with vigor. Just before he began the lesson he bent low over my desk. "Glenda, stay after class if you can. We have a lot to talk about."

I nodded. Yes, I thought, a *lot*. Christmas was over, and I couldn't avoid him any longer. If only my stomach would stop doing flip-flops. I didn't know what he was going to say to me or I to him. I was horribly nervous.

When the lesson ended at last and the classroom was empty, I remained sitting at my desk. My books were neatly piled on top in readiness for me to leave. Mr. Hartley walked toward me jauntily and sat down atop Alice Mackenzie's desk, alongside mine.

"Did you have a nice holiday, Glenda?"

"It was all right," I replied, not able to meet his gaze. "Did you?"

"Terrific." He slapped his palms together. "I was in Barbados the whole time. Don't tell me you haven't noticed my tan."

I realized that was why his teeth had appeared so exceptionally white. So he hadn't been in New York City where Cathanne had been. I'd let my imagination run away with me.

"Now," he said, "tell me what you've got scheduled in the way of rehearsals for this week."

"Nothing," I answered. "You told me to forget the scheduling until after Christmas. Remember? And I tried to tell you what Mr. Hauser said. But you . . ." The scene in the music room came back to me: David's impatience when I'd tried to explain about the rehearsal space, his asking me to bring him his coffee and then telling me to vanish, Cathanne throwing her arms around his neck, and then my fight with her while he'd stood by saying nothing.

Mr. Hartley leaned forward. "What's wrong, Glenda? This job too much for you? You know I believe in you. I still think you can handle it."

I got up from my desk abruptly, accidentally banging the side of my leg against the seat and jolting the pile of books. One book slammed to the floor.

David, still seated on Alice's desk, looked up at me in alarm.

"Of course, I can handle it," I said in a tense, high-pitched voice. "I . . . I can do anything I want to if I have a good enough reason. But . . . but I . . ." I stooped and picked up the fallen book.

David's eyes became somber, a less glittering blue.

"But you don't *have* a good enough reason. Is that what you're trying to say, Glenda?"

"I guess so," I answered a little more calmly. "This . . . this job wasn't what I wanted. Not really."

David nodded. "I guess I knew that. I never should have pressed you. My mistake."

"I should . . . shouldn't have taken the job," I stammered.

David stood up. "No harm done. I give you credit for knowing what works for you and what doesn't. And I release you."

His words and the seriousness in his voice came to me as a shock. I was grateful for his understanding, but I was also surprised and a little disappointed that he was so ready to let me go.

"We've been good friends, Glenda," David said in a warmer tone. "I hope we'll continue to be, even if you're not connected with the show."

I began to gather up my books with a mixture of relief and sadness. "Who'll you get for assistant director?" I murmured.

"Oh, I think I'll ask Robert Fry. He's anxious to help and he can get plenty of people to work on the lights and the sets for him."

For a moment I couldn't help wondering if Mr. Hartley had thought all this out in advance. Had he been expecting my resignation even before I'd realized I was going to give it to him?

A comical idea struck me. "But can Robert Fry make coffee that's H–O–T?" I was smiling for the first time.

Mr. Hartley winced. "I guess I've been an awful pest about that."

173

I felt like saying, "Why don't you learn to make it yourself?" But all I answered was, "You sure were!"

Just as I was about to leave the room, Mr. Hartley seemed to remember something. "Wait, Glenda," he called out, anxiously, "I've got something for you."

He dashed over to his desk and unclasped his briefcase. I watched him rummage around among his papers and pull out a small, slim book.

"Now, hold on a minute more. There's something I need to write in it."

He sat down at his desk, took out a pen, and wrote some words on the flyleaf. Then he gazed at me thoughtfully for a moment, holding the pen poised above the page.

Abruptly, David went back to his writing, closed the book, and handed it to me.

"You know what this is, of course. It's the prize you won for your sensational costume at the Halloween party. Sorry I've been slow getting it to you. I wanted it to be *this* book and it had to be special-ordered." He seemed truly apologetic.

I dropped my school books onto a nearby desk. The book Mr. Hartley had handed me was pale blue with a darker blue spine. The title in gilt letters read: *Sonnets from the Portuguese* by Elizabeth Barrett Browning.

"Oh," I said softly, with unconcealed pleasure. I wondered if I would find the love poem in it that I had picked out as my first assignment for Mr. Hartley.

"Open it," Mr. Hartley said. "See if you like what I wrote."

I opened the book to the flyleaf and read:

For Glenda—
Who metamorphosed before my eyes.
Happiness always,
David Hartley

I looked at him, and he must have read the puzzlement in my eyes.

"Metamorphose," he explained gently. "It means to change."

21

Dear Sara,

I haven't written you a letter since before Thanksgiving and here it is the middle of January. Can you ever forgive me?

That's how I began my long overdue letter to Sara in which I told her all about the events leading up to my quitting the show. On the last page, I wrote:

I guess, like Miss Esme said, I was just a victim of puppy love. But even if I *was* fooling myself a little in the way I thought Mr. Hartley felt about me, my false dreams really did work for me—up to a point. I'm just glad I knew when it was time to quit.

Right now I'm not losing much weight, but at least I'm not gaining any either. I guess it's going to be hard to lose twenty pounds without some very good reason, even if it's just a foolish but wonderful fantasy.

Who knows, Sara, maybe I'll just have to settle for being somewhere in-between, not fat but not really skinny either. And I'll have to learn to like myself the way I am and hope that other people will, too.

Of course, I'm going to Miss Esme's classes and jogging regularly again. In fact, after I seal this letter, I'll run to the mailbox over on the other side of Havenhurst with it. That's what I used to do. Remember?

I got into my jogging suit and started out in the January cold. The air was very still and my breath came in steamy puffs that seemed to hover around my head like smoke rings. The streets were deserted on this late afternoon in the dead of winter. Overhead the sky was a heavy grayish-white.

I was huffing and puffing, partly from the cold and partly from the extra weight I was running with. And Patty had been right about my losing my muscle tone when I'd suddenly stopped attending the dancercise classes. I ached all over again these days.

At last the mailbox came into sight at the end of the quiet residential street, and I began to slow down. I was just reaching into my inside pocket for the letter to Sara when I heard a whooshing sound at my side and the scrape and squeal of bicycle tires coming to a halt.

"He-e-e-y-y, Glenda."

I turned, startled.

"Gee, I've been trailing you for a couple of blocks. I called you. Didn't you hear me?"

It was Roddy. He was standing astride his bike at the curb beside me.

I stuck my finger into the close-fitting hood I was wearing to keep my ears from freezing.

"Guess not," I said, holding the hood away from one ear so I could hear better.

Roddy stood there looking at me with a thoughtful grin.

"What's up?" I asked, still panting a lot. "How come you were following me?"

Roddy dropped down onto his bike seat. He waved his arms. "No special reason. Just wanted to find out what's happening with you. Haven't seen you in a while."

"That's true," I agreed. It was odd how Roddy's class schedule was so different from mine that I almost never bumped into him in school. The last time, in fact, had been the day of the rehearsal in the music room when Roddy witnessed the fight between Cathanne and me.

"I'm just mailing a letter to Sara Mayberry," I said, holding up the envelope for Roddy to see. "You remember her."

"Oh, sure," Roddy said. "So you two are still good friends, huh?"

I laughed a little sourly. "No thanks to you. You tried to bust up our friendship lots of times during the year she lived in Havenhurst."

"Aw, come on, Glenda," Roddy coaxed. "Can't you let bygones be bygones? That stuff's ancient history."

I shrugged as I walked up to the mailbox and dropped in the letter. "Oh, maybe I can."

It *was* a long time ago, as Roddy said.

Roddy followed me, pushing his bike forward along the ground with his feet. "And you ought to forget all that other bad stuff, too, you know."

I gave the mail slot cover an extra bang just to make sure the letter had gone through.

"Oh, I'm forgetting it," I said. "I'm honestly glad I quit the show. And I'm getting to have more normal feelings toward Mr. Hartley now. I mean I don't adore him the way I used to when I sat looking at him in English class, and I don't despise him like I did after that day when he let Cathanne make me feel like a . . . a nobody. I really *have* changed. I think of him as I would any other teacher. Well, most of the time anyway."

Roddy kept staring at me with interest, but he didn't say anything.

"Oh, and another thing," I said, beginning to chuckle, "I heard something really juicy the other day. Well, anyway, it gave me a lot of satisfaction. Robert Fry told me that Cathanne comes to all the rehearsals now, even when she isn't scheduled for a run-through. And you know what she does? She makes Mr. Hartley his coffee in the teacher's room and she brings it to him. And, well, the other day it wasn't strong enough or hot enough, and he was in a bad mood anyway. And he *yelled* at her!"

In my surging glee, I actually began to pound Roddy's arm with both fists.

Roddy grabbed my mittened hands. He was smiling

179

broadly with understanding, but he wasn't laughing hard the way I was.

"Okay, okay," he said. I'm glad you got out from under. I told you that day that you should quit, even before Cathanne did her big scene on you. Only, listen Glenda, the stuff about the show wasn't what I meant really when I said you should forget the bad things."

"Oh, really?" I asked suspiciously. "What else should I forget?"

Roddy turned his bike around, got back on the seat, and placed one foot on the pedal. He looked like a racer about to take off in a hurry.

"Well," he said, grinning at me fiercely, "I'd like you to forget that I called you 'Jelly Belly.' Think you could do that?"

"Oh, *you!*" I exclaimed, shaking a fist at him. "I always *knew* you were the one. Why'd you lie and say you weren't?"

Before Roddy could give me an answer, we were both struck in the face by a sudden rain of chilling sleet. It slanted down from the sullen gray-white sky with the force of a cloudburst.

Roddy looked up, squinting against the hard-hitting icy needles. "You're not gonna run all the way home in *this,* Glenda. Listen, why don't you hop on my bike? I'll ride you."

I looked at him doubtfully.

"Come on," he urged. "I'm dead serious."

Maybe Roddy was right. Maybe this was a good time to forget about the past, about my sadly changed feelings for Mr. Hartley, about Cathanne's nastiness, about my silly fights with Patty, Mary Lou, my mother, everyone, even about Roddy's having called me "Jelly Belly."

At least Roddy had been honest with me and finally admitted it. And, surprisingly, at a time when I hadn't even asked him.

I got onto the back of the bike and wrapped my arms tightly around Roddy's waist to keep from falling off.

"Sure I'm not too fat for you?" I teased him over his shoulder.

Roddy began to pedal. "Nah," he said.

I looked down and watched his legs whirling faster and faster as he rode furiously against the driving sleet.

"You're not too fat, Glenda," Roddy assured me, turning his head briefly. "Not at all."

ABOUT THE AUTHOR

LILA PERL was born in New York City. Since acquiring a BA degree from Brooklyn College she has taken graduate courses at Teachers College, Columbia University and the School of Education at New York University. She has written more than thirty books, both fiction and non-fiction, most of them for young people. Many of her books were inspired by her two children as they grew up. Archway editions include *Pieface and Daphne* and *Me and Fat Glenda*. The author received so many letters asking about Glenda and suggesting diets and exercise programs, that she decided to write a sequel—*Hey, Remember Fat Glenda?*—to bring all her readers up-to-date on Glenda's accomplishments.

Ms. Perl is a full-time writer, but when she gets a chance, she enjoys traveling to exotic parts of the world; she has just recently returned from China. She lives in Beechhurst, N.Y., with her husband, Charles Yerkow, who is also a writer.

The Hopes,
the Fears,
the Problems
of the Young...
Jeannette Eyerly
Understands Them